A FIGHTING CHANCE

Praise for T.L. Hayes

Sweet Boy and Wild One

"I love novels that make you think and consider issues outside of your normal personal stratosphere. Trans issues are of deep concern all over the world, so I commend T.L. Hayes for tackling an issue and making it into a beautiful and positive romance that I will remember for a long time…I highly recommend this to all of the LGBTQI community and hope that reading the book not only gives you the heart flutter but that you also learn a bit more about how important Trans issues are. I'll be watching what comes next from T.L. Hayes and hope she continues the story into a sequel because this lesbian may have a little boy crush on Bobby, he melts hearts!"—*Les Reveur*

A Class Act

"What a beautiful, romantic and heart-warming love story! I really enjoyed being an onlooker in this well written and totally engrossing new relationship between Maggie and Rory."—*Inked Rainbow Reads*

By the Author

A Class Act

Sweet Boy and Wild One

A Fighting Chance

Visit us at www.boldstrokesbooks.com

A Fighting Chance

by

T.L. Hayes

2018

ISBN 13: 978-1-63555-257-7

This Trade Paperback Original Is Published By
Bold Strokes Books, Inc.
P.O. Box 249
Valley Falls, NY 12185

First Edition: September 2018

Credits
Editor: Ruth Sternglantz
Production Design: Stacia Seaman
Cover Design by Jeanine Henning

Acknowledgments

As always, the Bold Strokes team has my sincere thanks for continuing to publish my work. I'm glad they continue to take a chance with me and my story ideas, and I have plenty, so I hope to be working with them for a long time ahead. As always, Ruth Sternglantz does a great job making sure my words flow smoothly and that I am telling the best story possible. Thank you, Ruth, for your diligence on my behalf. Also, much thanks go to Jeanine Henning for the beautiful cover. She was able to take what was in my head and make it real, and it shines so well, Cassiopeia herself would be jealous.

As always seems to be the case, my main source of information for this novel, particularly in matters of kung fu, as well as the stray French translation, was my dear friend April Duncan. She just seems to know a lot about a lot, and I'm glad she does. She keeps me honest, she makes me laugh, and she is forever patient with my multitude of questions that usually start with the phrase "Current need: etc." Thank you, April, for your knowledge, and your willingness to share it with me.

There were delicate matters in this novel concerning C-PTSD and childhood trauma as well as suicide and other related issues to these topics. Some of them have touched my life on a personal level, but I am not an expert in any of these areas. I wanted my characters' experiences to be as realistic as possible, so I sought guidance from my friend, Maka Hansen, a sexual assault advocate with the Oklahoma City YWCA. Any truth I was able to represent for these matters is due to the information they provided; any inaccuracies are wholly my own doing. It should be noted that the reactions my characters have to their respective traumas and the treatments they seek are not meant to be representative of the whole. Meaning, I am not trying to speak for everyone who has suffered through these events, nor am I recommending any specific brand of treatment for all, only what was best for the characters I created and the outcome I foresaw for them.

I am not military, nor was I a military brat. Several times, I came upon questions that could not be answered simply by using government websites, though they were no great slouch in helping me with some of the rules and specific dates of things. For more obscure questions, I was able to get help from former military brat, and two-time military spouse, Suzanne Baker. She was right on the money with the things I put to her and she was quick with it, too.

A very brief part of this novel mentions Lawton, Oklahoma, home of Ft. Sill, a location I have my character Steve stationed at one point. I had questions about the local gay scene in Lawton in the mid-nineties, and Vicki Dilliard was quick to answer them for me. The information she was happy to provide me with was so rich in detail, I think she should write her own book. I would buy it.

I have several friends who work in academia, but one I go to more often than the others for questions about professorial life. Not only is she my token lesbian parent (which might come in handy later for future projects), but she is also my token professor friend. There's a moment in the text where I mention lizards. Lara LaDage is that reason. I appreciate all the insights she gives me about academia, a profession I respect and admire, and should probably stay away from. I don't know if I could sit through that many meetings without falling asleep or throwing things.

I have been fortunate to not suffer panic attacks, so I had to talk to others who have. I will not name them here, but I truly thank them for their candor and willingness to share. Again, how my character handles her panic attacks and the consequences thereto, are not meant to represent all those who deal with this issue on a regular basis or have in the past.

When it came to how to dress Steve for her first date with

Lou, I consulted the two most fashionable humans I know, Stefanie Heinrich and Lena Tenney. They are dapper beyond compare and know how to wear a suit better than anyone I know.

As I mentioned earlier, there are several delicate topics that are mentioned in this novel. I tried my best to handle them with care, and I hope I did my characters justice. If you or someone you know is under the age of eighteen and a victim of child abuse, one of the many available resources, besides local state hotlines and help centers, is the Childhelp National Child Abuse Hotline at 1-800-4-A-CHILD (1-800-422-4453). If you or someone you know is contemplating suicide and just needs someone to talk to, there are several options available. The National Suicide Prevention Lifeline is a 24/7 hotline which is part of a network of 161 crisis centers across the country, and they are always there to help. They can be reached at 1-800-273-TALK (8255). Also, there is the Crisis Text Line, which provides 24/7 crisis intervention for those contemplating suicide. They can be reached by texting 741741. For better understanding of C-PTSD, what it is, and how to live with it, *Complex PTSD: From Surviving To Thriving* by Pete Walker, as well as other articles by Walker, were invaluable tools.

And for the readers who continue to read me, as well as the new ones who have just found me with this book, thank you for your interest in my stories. And if you've found me in your local library, that makes me happy, as some of the topics I write about are underrepresented in public libraries, and I'm glad if they count me among their LGBT collections.

Feel free to reach out to me on Facebook at T.L. Hayes, or via my website at TLHayesweb.com. Watch the website for deleted scenes, song links, and short stories, and Facebook for new book release information, as well as event announcements.

For my favorite warrior—her armor may be scarred, but she keeps fighting. She gives me strength and she is my hero.

You didn't expect this, but it's yours.
Even though I take a step back, it
is only to touch the ground and lay
palimpsest at your feet

CHAPTER ONE

Lou Silver thought burnt orange was such an odd color choice for the walls of her favorite coffee shop. Granted, it gave the place warmth, but it also seemed almost too warm and maybe just a bit pretentious. She sat alone in the back at a table for two near a power strip with her laptop open and a cup of coffee beside her. She knew she was going to be there for hours, so she had ordered what she always ordered—a bottomless cup of Seattle dark roast, not because she was particularly fond of Seattle coffee, but because that was the darkest coffee they currently had on tap.

The conversation level in the café was never intrusive regardless of the size of the crowd, and it all blended into white noise for her. She was happy to be away from her office and the knocks on her door that were a constant distraction, office hours or not. She loved her job and was happy with the progress of her career. She was on tenure track at a big university in a good-sized town, just two hundred miles from Chicago, her favorite city and a place she escaped to as often as she could. But sometimes, the demands from the students became too much and she had to get away. She was sure there were students in the café—it *was* a college town, after all—but none of them were her students, so they left her alone.

She had brought her laptop with the sole purpose of writing her novel, the same one no one knew she was working on. Growing up, she had been a fan of Tolkien and fantasy novels in general and had always wanted to create her own world inhabited by the strange creatures of her imagination. In the world she was creating, people walked into each other's dreams and changed things for the dreamer, sometimes for the better, other times not—it depended on the dream walker and whether they were good or if they had been manipulated by an as-yet-unnamed force who was using them to do their bidding. The book was a special passion of hers that she had been writing and rewriting for years. She hadn't completed it yet, between life intruding on her writing time or just not being satisfied with the revisions. The book had been such a constant in her life that it had lasted longer than her previous two relationships and had even, barely, survived a flood. It was constant and invincible, it seemed to her, and she knew the book really wanted to be written, as odd as that might sound to some. Now her novel was reaching chapter twelve and her coffee cup had been refilled three times in the last two hours. She was thoroughly caffeinated but figured she would end up drinking at least two more cups before she left.

She looked up from her writing and noticed a man in uniform had taken the table in front of her. He was wearing army fatigues and khaki-colored boots and his sandy blond hair was cut in a high and tight that made his ears stick out. There wasn't a military base around for miles, so she figured he must be a student in the ROTC program on campus. When she realized she was staring at the back of his head she shifted her gaze back to her laptop and her mostly empty cup, thinking that if she was going to be this easily distracted, she should probably call it a day.

Just as she was packing everything in her satchel and was standing to leave, the young man in uniform stood too and smiled at her when he noticed she was looking. When Lou smiled back, she realized her mistake: the soldier wasn't a young man at all but a young woman. Over the girl's left breast pocket was emblazoned *US Army* and over the right was *Bolen*. She actually had the audacity to blatantly look Lou over and nodded and grinned. Lou tried not to roll her eyes at the girl's boldness. She had no desire to flirt with, much less date, someone who didn't even look old enough to drink. Lou just gave her a weak smile, then quickly left, lest she give the girl a chance to ask her out, which she would have to politely refuse, for many reasons. Just the same, it was nice to know she could still get such looks from girls half her age. It definitely did a lot for her ego, if not her libido.

Lou threw her satchel into the back seat of her Jeep Wrangler and climbed in behind the wheel. Her car was pushing twenty years old but she was reluctant to get a new one, even if she could now afford it. The blue Jeep was holding up well, despite how much she abused it. When she turned the key the Check Engine light came on and her mileage readout reminded her that she was desperately in need of an oil change. But her tank was full, and considering how much gas the Jeep ate, that was saying something. The satchel sat on the back seat amongst empty paper coffee cups from a fast food place near her little house and her gym bag. Seeing it reminded her that she needed to take it inside and wash the contents—she'd be teaching at the Wushuguan that weekend, and it wouldn't do to show up smelling like used sweat socks.

❖

With her gear slung over her shoulder, Lou was about to leave the Wushuguan after the class she taught on Saturdays when she heard one of her students call her name—a retired librarian in her sixties who wanted to learn kung fu for kicks, she had said, before laughing at her own joke. Lou had laughed with her, liking the older woman instantly. Now, at the sound of her name, Lou turned around with a smile. "Yes, Mrs. Adams?"

The tiny gray-haired woman was pulling a taller, younger woman along beside her. "Louise, I wanted to introduce you to my daughter. She just retired from the service, so I'll actually get to see her more often." Mrs. Adams smiled and then said, "This is Stephanie."

Stephanie looked Lou over. "Nice to meet you. Mom talks about you a lot. I mean, how much she likes your class."

Stephanie smiled, somewhat shyly, Lou thought. Lou checked her out as she was shaking her hand. She was about her height, so that would make her about five seven. She was slender and athletic looking with good definition. There was a lot of power in her handshake. Lou liked that show of strength. Her hair was cropped short, not a high and tight exactly, but close. Lou knew the military only required that enlisted women keep their hair neat and trim and pulled back, so the short style was all Stephanie's choice. Lou immediately pegged Stephanie as gay—not just because of her hairstyle, although some lesbian clichés were true, but for the way she had cruised Lou a few seconds ago. Stephanie apparently liked what she saw, which was flattering, but Lou couldn't say the same.

Butch women, no matter how much she appreciated them for their strength of character, their physical prowess, and their ability to fix things that she herself could not...well, she had never been attracted to them.

"Nice to meet you too, Stephanie. And"—she turned to Mrs. Adams—"I'm glad you're enjoying yourself."

"Oh, I am. You are such a good teacher. You have a lot of patience for clumsy old ladies like me." Mrs. Adams lightly touched Lou's arm in emphasis. Stephanie just looked indulgently at her mother.

"Mrs. Adams, you're not clumsy. We all learn at our own pace and you're doing very well. You'll be kung fu fighting in no time." Lou smiled at them both. Mrs. Adams was one of her favorite students.

"That's what I tell her, but she won't listen to me." Stephanie directed her words at her mother while glancing at Lou. "Mom, you just have to be more confident in your own abilities. You'll get it in time."

Lou laughed. "And that's what I tell her but it hasn't sunk in yet."

"With you two in my corner, maybe I can take on Rocky." Mrs. Adams did a fake fighting hand gesture and a kick, making Lou and Stephanie laugh.

"And you would probably win. He didn't know kung fu."

"Quite true. Well, it was good talking with you, but we need to get. I just wanted to brag about my firstborn."

"As you should." Lou bowed to Mrs. Adams, who returned the gesture, then turned to Stephanie. "And sorry I forgot to mention it earlier, but thank you for your service." She offered her hand.

Stephanie shook her hand and gave her another smile, this one with more confidence. "That's okay. It's almost hard to hear sometimes, as it isn't always meant sincerely, just something people say. But I think you actually mean it."

"I do mean it. My father was a veteran of two wars, and I've always had a deep respect for our troops, whether I believed in the war they were sent to fight or not."

Stephanie rolled her eyes. "Don't get me started. I agree with you. I love my country and was proud to serve it, and would die for it if I had to, but I wanted it to be for a good reason. I'm not the only person in uniform who feels that way. Listen to me—I said don't get me started."

"It's okay. I understand."

"If you two want to discuss politics," Mrs. Adams interjected, "do it some other time. We still have to stop by the store. See you tomorrow, Louise." Mrs. Adams smiled and waved, then grabbed her daughter's sleeve and made to walk toward the door, but Stephanie stayed where she was.

Stephanie looked at Lou and quickly said, "I would like that, actually. To do this again. Can I buy you a cup of coffee sometime? And you can call me Steve."

Lou hesitated. Stephanie seemed nice and she had been a bit lonely in the past year since starting the job at Prairieland State.

She wasn't in the market for a girlfriend, but someone to have coffee and talk politics with might be a welcome find. Why not? Sometimes coffee was just coffee, right? "Sure, I'm free Tuesday afternoons, if that works for you. And call me Lou."

Steve's grin got bigger. "Okay, Lou, that sounds good. How do I reach you?"

"Your mother has my number."

"Okay."

Mrs. Adams shook her head. "I can't take you anywhere. Are you done flirting with pretty girls now? I have things to do." Her pronouncement broke the sudden tension and made them all laugh.

"You say that like I do this all the time." Steve looked at Lou and declared, "I don't—do this all the time, I mean."

Lou just laughed. "I believe you. I think you should do as your mother says now. We'll talk later."

"Good-bye, Louise. Come along."

Mother and daughter left, but not before Steve got in one final smile at Lou. Lou shook her head and smiled back. Well, this was an interesting development.

❖

Steve was lost in thought as she drove her mother home. Her mother was perfectly capable of driving herself, but Steve knew she enjoyed this time they shared together. She stole a glance at her mother, who was looking out the window.

Her mother pointed to an empty storefront. "Did you see they closed the old Myer's Pharmacy? Ever since those chains came in, we've been losing them left and right."

"We didn't have that many family-owned drugstores to begin with." Just the same, Steve afforded the building in question a glance as they passed by. Sure enough, the windows were now dark and there was an abandoned look about the place.

Her mother turned to her with a look of mild reproof. "I

mean mom-and-pop stores in general, not drugstores specifically. It's just a shame, is all. It's been there since before I was born. Hell, since my grandmother was born. I hate that I have to use the new place. It feels wrong somehow."

"I'm sure it does, but things change. Whether you're ready for them to or not." Steve reached up and touched the Capricorn pendant on the necklace she wore. She fingered it a moment, then realized what she was doing and stopped. She forced a note of levity into her voice. "Well, at least the ice cream shop's still here. We could always stop in. I'll buy you a waffle cone." Steve smiled over at her mother.

"Stop trying to make me fat! I've lost twelve pounds since I started working with Lou, and I mean to keep it off."

"Really? Good job. Thank you for introducing me to her, by the way."

"Well, obviously your way wasn't working."

Steve said nothing, just grinned at her mother's words. After all, she couldn't deny the truth of them.

Her mother pointed a finger at her and declared, "You be nice to her. She's a great girl and you make sure you treat her with the utmost respect. 'Course, if you don't, I'm sure she could handle it. But I mean it, Stephanie."

"Jeez, simmer down. You know I always treat women with respect. You and dad taught me well. And yes, I agree, if I didn't, I'm quite sure she could put me on my back in no time at all." Steve's mind started to drift at the possibilities and she almost missed the turn onto her mother's street.

"Stop daydreaming about my kung fu instructor—you almost missed my turn. Child, I swear." She shook her head in exasperation, but there was a smile on her face.

"Oh, sorry." Steve made the turn just before they passed it and she admonished herself to focus. When they pulled into her mother's driveway, she didn't move to get out of the car. "Well, I guess I'll see you tomorrow morning. What's on the menu for tomorrow night, anyway?"

"Weren't you paying attention in the store? We weren't there but five minutes ago. I swear, when you've got a woman on your mind, that's all you can think about."

Steve chuckled at her mother's assessment. "What can I say? Lou's more interesting than pot roast."

"I would go with that, if you're looking for things to say to impress her. All women like to know they're more interesting than a cut of beef." Her mother winked at her.

Amused, Steve asked, "Is that how Dad captured your heart?" She knew the real story but liked to get her mother going.

Her mother put her head back on the seat and looked wistful. "I'll never forget the time he looked at me and said, *Lorraine, you are like the perfect filet mignon. Small and juicy and you always leave me wanting more.*" She signed at the memory. "That man had a way with words."

Steve gave in to the laughter, then pointed toward her mother's door and said, "Go, get out of my car!"

"What a way to talk to your mother." She *tsk*ed but that didn't stop her from leaning over and kissing Steve on the cheek. "See you tomorrow, sweets. Love you."

As her mom was climbing out of the car, Steve replied, "Love you too, crazy lady." Steve shook her head as her mother curtsied at her remark, then walked up to her front door. Steve stayed where she was until she saw that her mother was safely inside, then pulled out of the driveway and headed home.

CHAPTER TWO

Lou sat at Bill and Dix's dining room table, enjoying the pasta Dix had prepared, somewhat lost in thought. Bill was the first friend she had made in the theater department. When Charles, their dean, had introduced her as the new instructor at a department meeting, Bill had come up to her afterward to introduce himself and had invited her to dinner to meet his husband. She'd liked him immediately, and he and Dix had quickly become her favorite people in her new town. It wasn't long before they made her feel like family.

It was Tuesday and she had thought she would have heard from Steve by now, not that she was waiting by the phone or anything. She had just thought…Well, she didn't know what she thought. That Steve liked her, she guessed, and immediately felt like she was back in high school again, wondering if the cute girl in class liked her back, and wondering if, even as adults, we ever really grew out of the awkward phase. She had often thought that being an adult just meant learning how to cover up just how shy and awkward you were.

"Earth to Lou. Come in, Lou." Bill held a basket of rolls in front of Lou's face and was passing them back and forth.

Lou smiled back sheepishly and grabbed a roll from the basket. "Thanks."

"So what's got you so distracted, anyway? You've barely said a word since you got here, and you haven't even insulted my

cooking once. I'm starting to think you don't love me anymore."
Dix did his best to look offended and it made Lou laugh. "There's
our girl. So what's going on?"

Lou sighed. "I'm sorry. You're right—I have been terribly
remiss. Dix, your pasta is gummier than my ninety-two-year-old
grandmother, and the sauce is one step above ketchup. Happy
now?"

"I would be if you meant it. Why are you so distracted,
anyway?"

"It's nothing. Really." The men exchanged an all-knowing
look. "What? What does that look mean?"

Bill imitated her nonchalant cadence when he replied, "It's
nothing, really." Then he grinned. "Teasing!"

"Don't make me throw this roll at you. I wouldn't want to
hurt you."

Dix laughed. "Now there's an insult I can believe."

"Well, sugar, we couldn't help but notice your absence
since you got here. We know when something's up. The last
time someone was in this house looking like that…" Bill paused,
looking almost horrified. "Oh, please tell me you haven't fallen
for a student too? I love Rory to death, but I don't think I could
go through that again."

"What? No, I have not fallen for a student. They're all like
my kids—I can't think of them that way."

Dix said to Bill, while giving Lou side-eye, "No, but I think
you're on to something. I think she has a new love interest. Or
something. Maybe just a little afternoon distraction, perhaps?"

"No, I don't think so. Does she really seem like the type for
casual sex to you? No, if Lou likes someone, it's not casual." Bill
shook his head, studying her as if she was a problem to be solved.

Lou couldn't help it. She grinned at them, amused by them
trying to figure her out as if she was complicated math. "Would
you two like me to leave so you can discuss me in private?"

"No, no, that won't be necessary. We'll figure it out in time."
Dix waved a dismissive hand, then took a bite of his food.

"Far be it from me to ruin your fun, but I'm not having an affair, nor on the verge of one, as far as I know. I'll keep you posted. Why are you so interested in what passes for my love life, anyway?"

"Because we love you, sweetie, and we want you to be happy," Bill said.

"Uh-huh."

"And we find the mating habits of the North American lesbian quite fascinating. We haven't had one to study since Maggie left," Dix replied, trying and failing to keep a straight face.

"So is that the reason you've invited me over in the first place for the past year? You needed a new lesbian to observe?"

"You have to admit, it was rather nice of Charles to fill Maggie's seat with another lesbian," Bill said. "I appreciate his willingness to keep the queer status quo among the faculty. I shouldn't have to carry that burden on my own."

"Wait…are you implying I didn't get the job on the merits?" Lou teased.

"Depends. Are we talking your merits in your field or your merits in…"

"Bill, don't you dare finish that sentence!" Lou laughed. "Or I will show you how to kill a man with a dinner fork."

"Oh, don't kill him. The holidays are coming up. It would make celebrating so tacky," Dix playfully lamented.

Lou smiled at Dix and lowered her fork but not before Bill held up his hands and said, "I surrender."

"I notice how we have somehow gotten away from the fact that something or someone is on your mind. Enough to distract you," Dix noted.

Lou gave another sigh, this one in defeat. "Fine. You win. But there really isn't much to tell."

"Oh, let us be the judge of that." Bill grinned delightedly.

"Do I have a choice?"

"Not really, no." Dix smiled at her. "Go ahead, spill."

"Fine. I did meet someone over the weekend. She's the daughter of one of my kung fu students. Ex-military. Kinda cute and seemed to like me. I just don't know…"

"Nothing bad so far. What's the problem?"

Lou turned to Bill and shrugged. "I don't know. She's really butch, for one thing, and I've never been attracted to butch women. But also, the military thing is a turnoff. I mean, she's ex-military, but still. It's the attitude. I can't deal with the ultra-disciplined nature of people in the military."

"I've never heard you be so judgmental before. This is new." There was no teasing manner to Bill's words this time. Instead, he looked troubled.

Lou looked at him sharply. "It's just, it's a thing I have, okay? Can't I have one thing? I mean, I'm not normally a judgmental person, no, but I have hang-ups the same as anyone. Nothing wrong with that." Lou picked up her fork and looked down at her plate as she caught Bill and Dix exchanging worried expressions. The air in the room seemed to change, the joviality of earlier set aside.

Finally, Bill said, "Sure, honey, you're allowed to have hang-ups. You're right, we all do. But I don't think it was your hang-ups that made you so distant tonight." His voice was gentle. "Is it possible you like her, but something else is tripping you up?"

"I don't know, maybe. Plus, she said she would call. If nothing else, I hate that feeling of unrequited anticipation. You know what I mean?"

"If that's a fancy way of saying waiting by a phone that doesn't ring, yes, I do. It's a universal problem that we've all experienced at one time or another. And it sucks, but don't get so worked up about it. If she calls you, then great, see what happens. If she doesn't, then she obviously wasn't worth you stressing over it too much." Bill gave her a kind smile.

"You're right. You're absolutely right. Why should I be this upset over someone I'm not even sure if I would even go out with?"

"That's right." Dix smiled indulgently at her.

"Sorry, guys. I promise to be here with you for the rest of the evening. You will have my undivided attention." She waved her hands in front of her, as if making a declaration. "Besides, I would be totally remiss if I failed to mention the sorry state of this chicken." She grinned as she fell into the familiar routine of insulting Dix's cooking, a banter that they had been engaging in since she had first come to dinner, and something they both enjoyed.

"That's my girl." Dix raised his glass of wine and Lou her beer bottle, which she knew they only kept stocked for her, and they toasted. Lou held her bottle aloft to Bill and did the same.

❖

Just as Lou was getting into her Jeep after leaving Bill and Dix's place, her phone buzzed in her pocket. It wasn't the quick buzz of a message, but a continuous vibrating rhythm that indicated she was getting a call. She pulled the phone out of her pocket once she was settled and saw that the display read *Mrs. Adams*. She sighed as she pushed the talk button. With false cheer, she said, "Hello, Mrs. Adams, how can I help you?"

"First, you can call me Steve, as I asked you to the other day." There was humor in the voice and it made Lou smile in spite of herself.

"I should have realized you would use your mother's phone to call me."

"Wanted to make sure you would answer."

"What makes you think I wouldn't have answered?"

"Well, unknown number and all. And you seem like you might be the cautious type. I just figured…" Steve faltered.

Lou interpreted it as shyness and chose to find it endearing. "Well, whatever you figured, you were wrong," she said with humor. "So now that I have already done what I could to exceed your expectations, what else can I do for you?"

Steve chuckled. "I'm told you like a good cup of strong coffee, and I've heard buying someone a cup of coffee is a good way to get to know them."

Amused in spite of herself, Lou asked, "Do I even want to know what else your mother told you about me?"

"Only that you're some kind of professor at the college, a black belt, and the best teacher she's ever had for anything. And that I would be disinherited if I was a jerk to you. Not that I wasn't going to be on my best behavior anyway."

Lou put her fist to her mouth to stifle her smile, even though there was no one around to see it. "Tell her that if you *are* a jerk, she'll be the first to know."

"I'll let her know, she'll be so pleased." Then Steve said, "So, about that coffee...what's your favorite place?"

"It's a place near campus, Raphael's."

"I've seen it. Tell me, is it named after the artist or the Ninja Turtle?"

"Considering the amount of pretentiousness, I'm guessing the painter."

"Pity."

A part of Lou felt a little silly for having this conversation on Bill and Dix's driveway and hoped they wouldn't look out the window and see her still sitting there, but she wasn't going to drive away while on the phone. Leaving could wait. "Fan of the Turtles, are you?"

"The Turtles, not so much, but April O'Neil, very much. You know, you remind me a little of her."

There was an unmistakably flirtatious quality to Steve's voice that hadn't been there before, and Lou wasn't sure how to react to it. Again, she chose to be amused by it. "April O'Neil was a redhead in a horrendous yellow jumpsuit. I have neither red hair nor a horrendous yellow jumpsuit."

Steve laughed. "Well, my mother thinks you're a badass. Maybe Lara Croft would be a better comparison then."

"Your seeming obsession with female cartoon characters is

starting to become troublesome and makes me worry that I will not be able to live up to your expectations of badassery." Lou was definitely enjoying herself. She hadn't had a date she could joke around with in this manner in quite some time.

Steve laughed again. "Hey, Lara Croft was a video game character, so animated but not really a cartoon. And I think you're going to live up to all my expectations. You may even exceed them."

Lou took a breath. The flirting was getting to be a bit much for her and she immediately wanted to back away from the conversation. She sobered and asked, "So when did you want to meet for coffee?"

Steve said, "How about Thursday afternoon?" The flirtation was now gone from her voice, for which Lou was glad.

"Okay. I'm free after four."

"Four thirty then?"

"Okay. Sounds good. I'll see you there." Just as they hung up and before Lou could collect herself and drive away, she received a text from Bill.

Not that I'm trying to get rid of you, but why are you still in my driveway?

Smiling, Lou responded, *I had a phone call. Didn't want to talk and drive. Will be leaving now—that is, unless you wish to keep detaining me.*

Oooh, did Sgt. Hottie finally call?

LOL I never said she was hot, but yes she did. Can I go now?

She would have to be hot to be worthy of you, love. But yes, I suppose you can. Drive safe and keep me posted. Look up.

Lou did as instructed and saw Bill and Dix waving to her from their kitchen window. Laughing, she waved back, then replied, *Aw, thanks, you big softie.* Then, after throwing the phone into her center console and with one final wave at the boys in the window, she drove off, replaying the phone call in her head and trying to decide how she felt about the whole thing.

Chapter Three

Steve checked herself out in the mirror before she left for the café. She loved how her black Levi's fit her. She'd had them for years and they hugged her frame well, and their cut, along with her boots, gave her the appearance of being taller than she was. She had hesitated about wearing the black shirt, but it went well with the jeans and it was an old favorite. She buttoned the top button, then looked at herself, her eyes focusing on that top button. She thought about unbuttoning it, but after years of being in the military and adhering to dress code, leaving it unbuttoned felt sloppy, so she left it.

She turned her head left then right, checking out the work of the barber she had gone to that morning. It had taken her a while to find a barber who would cut women's hair. She had thought it was just a matter of preference, until the barber that morning informed her that most barbers just didn't have the proper license and could only cut men's hair. She was happy with the guy she found, even if the place was a new retro hipster place that did well to bring back the old-school barber motif, complete with old barber chairs, a tricolored pole, and old signage from a time when her grandfather had been a young man. No matter that her barber had a boy band flip on his own head, he seemed to know what he was doing and had given her a great buzz, leaving a little style to it so she didn't look as if she had just entered basic training.

She reached for her cologne, thinking she would dab a little something on her neck at the very least, then thought better of it. It was just coffee, not a night on the town. Maybe, if she was lucky enough to get Lou to agree to a night out, she would splash a little something on, but for the time being she stilled her hand and instead went back to fussing at the button. She put her hand up to it, thinking it still looked wrong somehow. It took her a moment to realize why, and she pulled the pendant out from under her shirt and kissed it, then let it fall to her chest on the outside of her shirt. She gave a relaxed sigh and finally smiled at her reflection.

"You got this."

Lou walked into the café at four twenty, thinking she would beat Steve there and have time to order her coffee and find a table, but she wasn't two steps in the door when she heard her name and looked to the right and saw Steve sitting on an overstuffed leather couch. *Great.* She wouldn't have the protection of a table between them. She gave Steve a small smile and a wave and walked over to her. Steve stood when Lou reached the couch and extended her hand, which Lou shook.

"Hi, Lou. I'm glad you're here. I was going to order you a cup of dark roast, but I didn't know how you take it and I wasn't sure how you'd feel about me ordering for you, so…" She suddenly looked unsure of herself as she fumbled for her words.

Lou bit back an amused grin and said, "No, that's fine. I'll be right back." She started to walk away, then stopped and turned, this time letting the smile come. "Oh, and for future reference, my preference is Colombian with skim milk and maple syrup, but failing that, I'll take whatever dark's on tap." Then she turned and went up to the counter, not watching to see Steve's reaction. When she returned a few minutes later, Steve rose again and didn't sit back down until Lou did. Well, that was kind of endearing. Nothing wrong with good manners.

"So, you must tell me, Professor Silver, just what are you a professor of, anyway?" Steve shifted on the couch so she was facing Lou, and she propped her right foot on her left knee.

Lou tried to keep focused on her face, but she'd be lying if she said Steve wasn't attractive. Steve was taller than Lou and lithe looking, with long legs. When Lou had told the boys that Steve was butch, she wasn't joking. Buzz-cut blond hair, black men's Levi's, combat boots, and a black button-up men's shirt completed her ensemble for today. The only color she wore was a simple silver chain with a silver Capricorn pendant, not the goat symbol but the one that Lou always thought looked like 7 and 6 put together. Lou held her coffee with both hands and blew across the mug. "Well, my main focus is stage combat, but I teach other classes in the department. Most of which are cross-listed between several majors."

"So your reputation as a badass is not unfounded, then." Steve said it as a statement that brokered no argument.

"Mm-hmm, but one I did not get easily."

"Being a badass usually doesn't come easily."

"What about you? What was your specialty in the military? Where did you earn your stripes?"

"Interesting way of putting that. I was a PT instructor. Maybe we should spar sometime."

Lou narrowed her eyes at Steve. "You have an interesting way of flirting."

Steve laughed out loud. "What can I say? I guess I'm not that far removed from playground days."

Lou wasn't as amused by the conversation as Steve appeared to be. "I've never really found violence much of a turn-on, to be honest." Her words were spoken softly but with a lot of power. She cleared her throat and looked away.

Steve seemed to pick up on Lou's shift in mood and looked at Lou worriedly. "Did I say something wrong?"

Lou exhaled and forced a smile. "Not really, sorry. I know you probably didn't mean it the way I took it. I just meant that usually when people invoke playground flirting, they're referring to the little boy's habit of hitting the girl he likes and then running away. Never cared much for that scenario."

Steve looked stricken. "Oh, I see. I'm sorry. I'm really not violent—I mean, I like to spar in the ring, that's all. I promise." They didn't say a word for a moment, just shared a look. Finally, Lou broke it by looking down at her mug.

After a moment she looked back up and said, "So, you're a Capricorn."

Visibly startled, Steve said, "What?"

Lou pointed to Steve's necklace.

Steve reached up and touched the symbol and suddenly looked sad. "No...um, no. I wear it for someone else."

Not sure about the shift in mood, Lou said, "I'm sorry. I didn't mean to trouble you."

"No, it's not your fault." Steve paused a moment, then she said quietly, "My first love was a Capricorn. I wear it in her memory."

"Her memory?"

"She died a couple years ago. We were going to get married." Steve looked down at her hands and swallowed.

Lou reached out and put a hand on Steve's knee. "I'm so sorry. You can talk about it if you want."

Steve put her hand over Lou's, then looked her in the eye and gave her a brave smile. "Nah, not today. Not exactly good first date material. Maybe another day, though."

Trying to tease, Lou asked, "Wait, this is a date? I thought we were just meeting for coffee. If I'd have known, I would have made more of an effort in my clothing choices." She had come straight from campus and she had had a combat class today. She had changed out of her workout clothes to her street clothes, olive-green cargo pants, a black blouse with three-quarter sleeves, and loafers. She hadn't had the time to shower, which she regretted. But she was the one who had set the time, knowing full well that would be an issue. She had only herself to blame.

"Well, if this isn't a date, I got a haircut this morning for nothing."

Feeling devilish, Lou asked, "May I?" and raised her hand partway.

Steve looked confused for a moment, then understanding dawned and she laughed. "Sure, go ahead." She leaned forward a bit and inclined her head.

Lou put her hand on the side of Steve's head and rubbed the short blond prickles of hair. They looked like they would be sharp but they were as soft as down. Lou's fingers lingered a moment too long and Steve raised her eyes but not her head and smiled. Lou broke contact and leaned her arm on the back of the couch but drew one leg up under the other, so they were still close enough to touch. Lou rested her cup on her foot. She didn't know what was happening, but she thought she was okay with it.

They talked for a few more hours, from the mundane to their views on a variety of topics, laughing together several times. After she figured she had drunk a pot of coffee, Lou realized it was time to go. "I should go—it is a school night, after all."

"Aw, okay. I understand. Walk you out?"

"Sure." They set their cups on the coffee table in front of them and stood to leave.

Steve walked Lou to her car and stood there awkwardly with her hands in her pockets. "I would like to see you again. The conversation was wonderful, and I'd be lying if I said I didn't like being petted." She raised her eyebrows comically and Lou laughed.

She was doing that a lot, Lou realized, and was glad of it. "Okay. You can take me to dinner on Saturday if you're free." Lou had no plans on Friday but she thought she needed a break before she saw her again.

"My old line used to be *The only thing that could keep me from having dinner with you would be a declaration of war*, but that line won't work anymore."

"A simple *I'm free* works for me."

Steve gave a small bow, but it was a courtly bow and not a martial arts one.

Lou hid a smile.

"As you like. I'm free. Pick you up at seven?"

Lou bowed in the way she was used to with a big smile and mimicked Steve's words. "As you like." Then they were both giggling. "Good-bye, Steve."

"Good-bye, Lou." Steve stood there until Lou got in her car and was buckled in, then waved as she pulled away. In her rearview mirror Lou saw Steve stay on the sidewalk for a minute more before walking away.

CHAPTER FOUR

On Fridays Lou was lucky enough not to have any classes, so she used that day to catch up on her grading and class prep to—at least in theory—free up her weekends, when she taught her kung fu classes, relaxed some, or met up with friends. And now, maybe date again. She mentally chastised herself not to get ahead of herself and think there was going to be anything more beyond one date. A lot could happen on a date and not all of it good. *Just relax, Lou, and take it as it comes.*

She was pulled out of her reverie by her office phone ringing and she answered automatically. "Dr. Silver speaking."

"Hey, Lou, how's it going?" It was Rachel, a former student, now a friend, who had graduated the past May. She and Bobby, her boyfriend, had moved out of state as soon as they'd been able, hoping to find a community more open to trans people. As much as Lou was sad to see them go, she understood why they'd felt the need to leave.

"Rachel, it's good to hear from you. I'm wonderful. How's life in the Land of 10,000 Lakes?"

"Like buttah."

Lou groaned. "I see it's done nothing for your sense of humor."

"Yeah, Bobby said he thinks my humor froze to death."

Lou smiled at the mention of the young trans man. "How is the sweet boy?" Before they left, Bobby had been the target of anti-trans violence. He had been hospitalized for a while but thankfully his injuries healed.

"He's good. Complains about the cold. I told him to suck it up and deal—it's not even winter yet. He says he's practicing for when it is. Oh, he told me to tell you he's started classes again. Says he wants to teach music composition, of all things." Lou could hear the pride in Rachel's voice, despite her flip words.

"That's great. Tell him I think that's wonderful and I wish him well. What about you? Found a job in the theater yet?"

"Yeah, sorta. Not my dream job, but I have a steady gig. Doing a little stage-managing, a little casting, whatever they need. Hell, I'm even learning lighting, just in case."

"You can never learn enough in the theater. You should know how all of it works."

"Yeah, Dr. Baskin used to say something similar. I'm trying. What about you? Torturing any more kung fu students?"

Lou smiled. "Only on the weekends."

"Aw, that's too bad. Others need to know the joy of your wrath." Rachel laughed.

Amused, Lou asked, "When was I wrathful?"

"Okay, not wrathful as such, but how about displeased?"

"You may find this hard to believe, but I was never displeased with you. You were one of my best students, in both fields. How could I be displeased with you? That doesn't mean you weren't trying at times." Lou smiled at the memory of all the times Rachel had challenged her in the classroom. She had been a smart-ass but Lou saw through that facade and saw the student who really wanted to learn and do well. The fact that she had cared enough to challenge Lou's authority was proof of that, Lou felt.

Rachel was silent a moment. Then, "Wow, thanks, Lou."

"You are very much welcome. Are you planning a visit anytime soon?"

"Ah, yeah, at Thanksgiving. His mother invited me to their house for the holidays."

"Wow." Up until the attack, Bobby and his mother had been

on the outs because she had had trouble accepting his transition, but once she'd almost lost her youngest child, she reexamined her priorities. "She must be really coming around, then."

"She's trying. She still slips on his gender sometimes but Bobby's patient. She's no longer doing it on purpose, and, as he says, as far as she knew, she had a daughter for twenty-five years, so it's going to take some getting used to. The fact that she's willing to try is enough for him."

"That's a good attitude to have. I'm happy for you both. I know I'm no longer your teacher, but you must come and see me while you're here."

"You're not going out of town?"

"No, my parents are both gone and I don't have any siblings, so I'm going to be staying in town, celebrating with friends." Bill and Dix threw what they called an orphans' Thanksgiving for their friends who either no longer had living parents to go home to or who had been rejected by them. She had been happy to be included last year and was looking forward to going again.

"Oh, okay, good. And yes, I don't think the sweet boy will allow me to be in the same town with you and not see you. You know he has the biggest crush on you, right?"

Lou laughed. "I'm sure that's not true. That boy loves you."

"Oh, I know, but that doesn't mean anything. He has a great respect for strong women, as should be obvious."

"You have a point there."

They talked for some minutes more, and before hanging up they made plans to get together over the coming holidays, which would be upon them in less than a month. When they finally disconnected, Lou couldn't stop smiling. Rachel hadn't just been one of her favorite students—she was one of her favorite people. Teachers weren't supposed to have favorites, the same as parents, but of course, they did. The trick was not to let the other students know who the favorites were, while still encouraging the favorites, who were usually the favorites because they were the ones who worked the hardest. Rachel had been no exception.

❖

Lou walked into her session with Mrs. Adams with a smile on her face. She couldn't help it; she was seeing Steve later and she had been in good spirits all day. She set her water bottle and towel down on a table off to the side of the mat, well away from the activity they were about to engage in. She took a sip of her water as she waited for Mrs. Adams and brushed back a curl that had escaped her hair clip. She loved her curls but they had a mind of their own, especially on humid days, and today had been one of those days.

When Mrs. Adams came in she smiled big and waved at Lou. She had her own towel and bottle of water she sat next to Lou's. She elbowed Lou lightly on the arm and winked. "So, if you and Stephanie work out, will I get a family discount?"

Surprised, Lou laughed. "Mrs. Adams, you should know I don't play favorites."

"Not even for your future mother-in-law?"

Lou grinned. "I had no idea you were a meddling yenta."

"I'm not, actually. Maybe a touch of a matchmaker, but a gossipy old woman? Nah."

"So you're not denying that you are trying to matchmake?" Lou raised an eyebrow.

Mrs. Adams laughed. "Well, I think Steve's doing just fine on her own, but anything I can do to help. You would be a fine addition to the family."

Lou felt her cheeks going warm as she said, "Thank you. But let's see how the first date goes before we start *setting* a date, shall we?"

"Too true. Besides, isn't it the second date when lesbians get serious? Hear tell anyway." Mrs. Adams was wearing a mischievous smile.

"Not this lesbian." Lou nodded to the mat. "Come on, time to go kick some butt."

Mrs. Adams bowed to Lou even though they weren't on the mat and it wasn't required. "Yes, Sifu." Then she waited for Lou to take her position before she followed.

As Lou began to put Mrs. Adams through her warm-up, it became harder and harder not to think of Steve, since Mrs. Adams had brought her up. Lou had been doing a great job of not thinking about her up until then, trying to focus on the session ahead, as Mrs. Adams deserved her full attention.

She thought about the text Steve had sent on Friday. It was sweet and she hadn't been prepared for that. *Looking forward to tomorrow. And hopefully many tomorrows. The feel of your fingers in my hair was lovely.*

Lou had been sitting in her office when it had come through, sometime after the call from Rachel, and she sat and stared at her phone for several minutes, alternating between smiling, and looking at it in wonder, not sure how to respond. Finally, after having given it some thought, she responded with, *Yes, to tomorrow. And if you play your cards right, I might pet you again. We shall see.* She had thrown her phone on the corner of her desk with a smirk.

Flirting wasn't something she was good at, and so she didn't do it often. Plus, flirting always came off as not terribly genuine to her, and being genuine was something she always strove to be. But she liked Steve's playfulness and she reasoned she wasn't so much flirting, as being honest. She *had* liked touching Steve. She thrived on touch and when she touched Steve just that little bit, she had had the urge to continue, letting her fingers linger. Maybe tonight she would get the opportunity to touch some more.

When the session was over, she and Mrs. Adams bowed to each other, and once they left the mat, the mischievous smile returned to Mrs. Adams's face.

"If my daughter can distract you this much before your first date, then I have high hopes for the future."

"And what makes you so sure it was Steve that had me distracted? It could have been my job."

"It never has been before. I know what I know."

"Uh-huh. I'm sure you'll hear a full report later, so you don't have to wonder, of course."

Mrs. Adams scoffed. "You think that child tells me everything about her love life? I can't say for sure how many girlfriends she's had, as I've only met the one." Suddenly, she looked sad and troubled and her smile faltered.

Lou noticed but didn't feel it was right to question it. Instead, she smiled gently. "Maybe that girlfriend was the only one who mattered."

Mrs. Adams looked relieved. "Yes, I believe you're right." Suddenly she gathered her towel and water bottle and said, "Well, I can definitely say there is nothing wrong with my daughter's taste. You are a bright, beautiful, fierce woman, and I really do hope things go well for both of you tonight." Mrs. Adams extended her hand.

Surprised, Lou shook it. "Thank you, Mrs. Adams. That means a lot."

"And you let me know if my daughter doesn't treat you with respect. She knows I'll use some of my mad ninja skills on her if I have to."

Lou laughed. "I will remind her."

"Good. See you tomorrow." Mrs. Adams started to walk away, then stopped and, with a twinkle in her eye, said, "You know, she's my only hope for grandchildren." Then she winked.

Incredulous, Lou just stood there in shock as Mrs. Adams walked away laughing.

Lou fussed with her curls, which she had decided to clip back. She had toyed with the idea of leaving her hair down altogether, but just the thought of constantly having to push it out of her face annoyed her. She never wore makeup, except on stage, but she did apply a little lotion to her face. Her mother, who also never wore makeup, had told her that moisturizing was the healthy thing to do. Simple silver hoops dangled from her ears and a charm bracelet that had belonged to her mother, containing a tourmaline charm, her mother's birthstone, adorned her wrist. She had loved it since she was a child because it had always reminded her of watermelon. She wore it when she was feeling playful. She didn't own much jewelry. She didn't have much occasion to wear it—jewelry didn't really mesh with stage fighting and martial arts.

She had thought a long time about what to wear, which was unusual for her, even on dates. Normally, she had no problem just grabbing something from her closet and feeling fine in it, but she wanted to take extra care tonight. As she was picking out a pair of black slacks, she had to ask herself what happened to the woman who, just a few days ago, sat at Dix and Bill's table and told them she wasn't even attracted to Steve, that she wasn't her type? She muttered, "I should work on not being this easy," then chuckled to herself as she finished getting dressed.

Next came the choice of blouse. Lou was usually fine in T-shirts, feeling they were right for most occasions, but she did own a few nice blouses that she brought out once in a while. The question was, black or add some color? She stood in front of her open closet door, arms crossed, chewing on her right thumbnail. Realizing that she was reverting to a childish habit, one she used to get yelled at for, she dropped her thumb and stood facing her clothes with her hands on her hips. Just as she was about to give up and text Bill, knowing he would know what to tell her, she heard his voice in her head. *Always go with color, unless you're going to a funeral or a cocktail party. This is a date, not a wake, shine a little!* Chuckling to herself at the thought, she grabbed a turquoise blouse out of the closet and put it on, then checked herself in the full-length mirror on her closet door. Her honey-blond curls were off her face but there were always a few that escaped and rested on her forehead. Her small wire-framed glasses made her look like the academic she was, but she couldn't do anything about that. Her smile was uncertain, almost shy, and she realized she was nervous. She took a deep breath, exhaled, and said to her reflection, "You got this." Before she could fuss any more, her doorbell rang, right on time. Of course.

When she opened the door, she saw Steve standing there with her hands crossed in front of herself, with her head cocked to the side and a small smile that got bigger once Lou was fully in view. "Hello, you look absolutely lovely."

Lou flushed. "Thank you. You're not so bad yourself."

"I clean up nice."

Clean up nice was an understatement, Lou thought. From head to toe, Steve was dapper—that was the best word Lou could think of. She was in a tailored charcoal-gray suit, shiny patent leather loafers, a crisp white shirt, and a gray and black paisley patterned tie, accessorized with a silver tie clip, all of which served to make her buzzed blond hair even more noticeable. Who was she kidding? Lou thought. *Steve* was noticeable. Lou swallowed and was sure Steve noticed because she grinned at her. Recovering, she said, "Yes, you do. And I suddenly feel underdressed." Nervously, Lou touched her blouse at her throat.

Smiling, Steve reached out and took that hand. "No, you look lovely, as I said. Now relax and believe that, and we shall go out and have a wonderful time." Suddenly, Steve bowed and kissed Lou's hand.

Lou chuckled, though not unkindly. "You are really good at this charm thing."

"Thank you, but, to be fair, I have to work at it. Ready?"

Lou nodded and stepped out on her porch, locked her door behind her, and rested her hand on the arm Steve offered. As they walked to the car, Lou said, "Anything worth doing is worth doing well. Nothing wrong with practice." Steve escorted Lou to her side of the car and opened the door for her. Lou smiled. She had never been on a date with a gentleman butch before, mainly because she had avoided dating butches.

When she got into the driver's seat, Steve said, "Which is why you are a badass ninja warrior and I am merely an amateur in the ring."

Lou laughed at the compliment. "Well, I do have a set of special skills," Lou said with humor.

Steve narrowed her eyes in Lou's direction and asked with the same humor, "Do you? Sounds intriguing and something I should know more about. Maybe even sexy." Steve's voice took on a lower register.

Lou was glad it was dark out, because she was sure she was blushing. "If you find the ninja pajamas—as my former student Rachel calls them—sexy, then there is something seriously strange about you. They're baggy and not at all flattering."

"I wasn't talking about your ninja clothes, just your skills, though I have a feeling they are sexy when you wear them."

"Wow, you are way better at flirting than I am. You must have had more practice than me."

"Ah, not so much as you would think. Not to sound cocky, but a butch in uniform is still a butch in uniform. Sometimes I didn't have to work for the attention, because the uniform did it for me. I only work at it when it matters." She smiled pointedly at Lou.

"I will take that for the compliment it was intended."

"Good."

"You know, you haven't told me where we're going. Are you planning on keeping it a mystery till we get there?"

"I thought about it. But if you really want to know, I thought I would take you to dinner and then we can figure it out from there. Maybe go for a walk. Find somewhere to keep talking. I didn't want to overplan."

"I appreciate that. I like the idea of making it up as we go."

They shared a smile and didn't say much for the rest of the drive to the restaurant, which turned out to be a French steakhouse Lou had been wanting to try since she had moved to town last year but hadn't had an excuse to visit.

When they pulled up, Lou noted, "You would think with a name like La Petite Vache, they would only serve veal."

Steve laughed out loud at Lou's joke. "Let's hope not. I was hoping for a nice steak."

"Let's go find out."

They did indeed serve steak, and there was plenty of conversation and more light flirting, mostly from Steve. Lou had decided to refrain, since flirting was outside her skill set. But that didn't mean she wasn't enjoying Steve's charming efforts. Steve continued being the perfect gentleman—holding doors, pulling out her chair, and letting her go first. All the things that Lou had always told herself she couldn't stand, since she could do all of those things for herself. She was not a helpless female who needed someone to do things for her. But when Steve did those things, Lou was able to see the respect behind each gesture and appreciated them in that vein.

When the meal was over, Steve turned to Lou and asked, "So where would you like to go?"

Lou thought about it for a moment, then smiled as a thought occurred to her. "How about the little pond on campus? There's a walking path around it and it's well lit. Even at night it's very pretty."

Steve looked surprised. "Well, that does sound nice. Okay, let's go there."

When they reached campus, she directed Steve to the visitors' parking lot, and then they made their way to the little pond, which Lou had only recently discovered had a name. Someone with an amazing gift for hyperbole had named the little man-made hole in the ground Lake Van Horn, after a former college president whose wife had insisted they name it after her husband. She had gotten her way. Now her husband's name lived on in the form of a small picturesque pond where young couples walked around holding hands, watching the sun set, feeding the ducks. Lou knew that Rachel and Bobby had had more than one romantic moment at that pond. Maybe there was something to its purported magic. Lou hoped it worked for her.

She and Steve began a casual stroll, hand in hand. Being there with Steve was *pleasant*—that was the word that kept coming to mind. Their conversation was light but not strained, just as it had been in the café when they had met for coffee. Steve minded her manners and never once tried to overstep by making a move that Lou might not welcome. Totally not what Lou had expected. And she chastised herself for her preconceived notion of what butches were like. She had a brief moment of regret about the women she had turned down over the years simply because she had expected them to be a certain way. But, not one to dwell on the past or things she couldn't change, Lou put that thought out of her mind and tuned back to the woman at her side. She was glad she had decided to judge Steve on her own merits and not against what she expected her to be.

When they pulled up at Lou's little house, Steve quickly got out of the car to hold the door for her. Lou waited for her to do so, then smiled at her as she stood and then took Steve's arm as they walked up to her door. At her doorstep, she turned around and said, "I had a wonderful time."

"Me too. You are a wonderful dinner companion. And you were right—the lake was a great location."

"You do know that I'll have to report to your mother tomorrow?" Lou asked with humor.

Steve laughed. "I know. I'm going to get it when I get home. She'll want to know everything."

Lou reacted in mock horror. "Oh no!" Then she chuckled.

Steve stepped closer. "Don't worry, we haven't done anything that would scandalize her. Not yet, anyway." Steve leaned in for a kiss good night and Lou responded by kissing her back and putting her hand on Steve's chest. Just as the kiss was growing in intensity, Steve stepped back.

Lou licked her lips, then looked down for a moment, and

then looked into Steve's eyes. Almost whispering, Lou said, "We don't have to tell her everything."

"No, no, we don't." Steve stepped back and suddenly looked awkward again, especially when she slipped her hands in her pockets. "I will definitely call you. I would like to go out with you again."

"Yes, absolutely." They both stood there for a moment, and then Lou realized she should say good night before she grabbed Steve and made a scene on her porch. She smiled. "Good night, Steve."

"'Night, Louise." Steve sighed, then left Lou's porch, and Lou let herself into her house and closed the door behind her.

That had gone surprisingly well. Considering her recent dating track record, which had been less than stellar, Lou appreciated the evening for what it was and hoped it really would be the start of something good.

Chapter Five

The next morning when Steve woke up and threw the sheet off, her first thought was of Lou and she smiled. The date had gone well and she hoped it was the start of more to come. As she stretched, she remembered the feel and taste of Lou's lips, the little smiles she caught Lou giving her from time to time, and the little almost unnoticeable scar on the bridge of Lou's nose that she figured Lou had earned somewhere in her career. The old adage was true: chicks did dig scars, and she wondered how Lou had gotten it. Just what sort of shenanigans had she been up to, to cause it?

Still smiling, Steve stood and went into the bathroom. When she finished in there, she quickly got dressed in sweats, thinking she would get a quick workout in before she had to pick her mother up so she could get hers. She walked into the garage that she used as a gym, went to the wall that held her bikes, and pulled down the one for in-town riding, then took a helmet off the wall. That was when she realized she'd forgotten her water bottle, so she went back inside to fill one up, then returned to the garage and rolled her bike out the side door into her driveway, mounted, then secured the helmet. Once she was set, she biked out of her driveway, taking a left turn. It was early on a Sunday morning, so the roads were clear and the kids weren't out yet. Further down her street, a dog came running up on her back tire, scaring her, but he just seemed happy to run alongside her and didn't approach, so she deemed him no threat. He lost interest after a couple of blocks and walked off happily in the direction he had come.

Steve kept going. She had in mind that she wanted to do a twenty-five mile trek through town. Easy enough, and something she knew she could do in about an hour and a half, give or take a few minutes. The route she had in mind took her past the university, though not the side the pond was on. Still, just seeing the spread-out campus, with its tall buildings and shady paths, made her think of Lou and the night before, but she quickly pushed those thoughts aside. She didn't want to get sidetracked. She was just grateful that the campus was quiet on Sunday mornings and there was little to no traffic. The campus bus didn't even run on Sundays. But there was still enough traffic from those who lived in the neighborhood next to the campus that she had to pay attention.

When Steve finally got home, she checked the clock on the microwave while she rinsed out the water bottle and left it in the strainer to dry. She still had time to shower and change before she picked up her mother to take her to kung fu practice. She really hoped she would get to see Lou again. She smiled when she remembered Lou referring to her kung fu pajamas the night before. She had yet to see her in them—Lou always changed before she left the gym.

❖

Lou walked into her session with Mrs. Adams running a little behind, which was unusual for her. She had lingered in bed after she woke up, then took a long leisurely shower. She had been in no hurry to leave the house, partly because she didn't feel as if she was up to all the self-disclosure she thought Mrs. Adams might ask for. It wasn't that she minded the teasing so much, just she didn't discuss her personal life with very many people, and Mrs. Adams, being her student as well as her date's mother, made the prospect even more awkward.

As soon as she saw Mrs. Adams, who was standing off the mat, drinking some water and looking happy, Lou smiled apologetically. "I'm sorry I'm late, Mrs. Adams. I can stay later if need be to make sure you get your full session."

"That's fine, dear. You're allowed to be human every now and again."

"Well, human is one thing, but there's no excuse for my lateness and you have my apologies. Shall we get started?"

With gusto and determination, Mrs. Adams declared, "Yes, let's do it."

Steve followed her to the mat, grateful Mrs. Adams hadn't insisted on talking about her date the previous evening, though she was aware that Mrs. Adams was *probably* waiting until after the session, which kind of put Lou on edge a bit in anticipation. Lou resigned herself to the inevitable and tried to put it out of her mind and focus on the session at hand. She had better success than she'd had the day before with that and was glad. After the final bows, Lou left the mat and went for her water bottle, and Mrs. Adams followed.

Mrs. Adams grabbed the small towel she had next to her water and wiped the sweat off her face and neck, then took a drink. She favored Lou with a warm smile. "It seems things went well. I'm glad."

Guarding her expression, Lou looked across at Mrs. Adams over her own water bottle and said cautiously, "It did, yes. It was a fun evening."

"You know, if I was in your shoes, I wouldn't want to tell the nosy old lady anything either, and that's perfectly all right. Don't worry about me. I really do stay out of my daughter's love life. It's just never been this close to home before. I couldn't help teasing you."

Lou instantly relaxed. "Oh no, that's fine. I can take a well-natured tease. It's not you, Mrs. Adams—I just try to keep my work and personal lives separate, is all."

"Well, in that case, if you and Steve become a couple, I'll

invite you to dinner and then you can spill in the comfort of my dining room."

Lou laughed. "I'm not sure I would find it so comforting if you plan to grill me."

"Oh, you wouldn't be on the menu, dear...at least, not mine."

Had Steve's mother meant what she thought she meant? Lou couldn't think of an appropriate response. "Don't look so shocked, dear. You know what they say about librarians."

"What do they say about librarians?"

"Sleep with a librarian, you might learn something." Again, Lou was speechless. "Where do you think Steve got her sense of humor from? Her father, bless his soul, was a serious man. One of us had to make inappropriate jokes."

Recovering, Lou said, "I learn something new about you every day, Mrs. Adams."

"Good, keeps you on your toes." Mrs. Adams's tone sobered when she said, "Don't worry, I'm not going to make you tell all. I'm just really glad it went well, and I hope it's the start of good things to come for both of you. You both deserve it."

Lou's tone softened and she said, "Thank you, Mrs. Adams."

"Oh, for crying out loud, if you keep calling me Mrs. Adams, I'm going to brain you, Sifu." She bowed but winked to show she was teasing. "From here on out, you will call me Lorraine, and I don't want to hear any protests. Got it?"

"I'll do my best. See you next week." Lou gave her a parting smile, then picked up her things and left, smiling to herself and shaking her head.

❖

As Lou drove home, she was thinking about many things: her smelly clothes in the back seat, the coffee cups she really needed to throw away, how great it would be to see Rachel and

Bobby again, and Steve. Though she was doing her best not to think of Steve. It had been one date, after all, that might or might not lead to more, with someone she still couldn't even say for sure why she was attracted to her, good looks and charm notwithstanding.

Just as she took a left onto Circle Court, into the cul-de-sac where her little house sat, her phone buzzed from the center console. Two quick buzzes told her it was a text message. She ignored it until after she pulled into her driveway and cut the engine, then she unbuckled the seat belt with her left hand while reaching for the phone with her right.

It was a text from Bill. *You must tell me ALL the details!*

She laughed out loud, then responded, *Gossip queen!*

Is there any other kind?

You're such a cliché.

I can live with that. Come to dinner tonight and tell us everything. I'm making steaks!

She grinned. *Okay, but only for the food! You're not getting a thing out of me!*

Well, you're no fun at all.

She was laughing as she got out of the Jeep. She was two steps away when she stopped, snapped her fingers and doubled back, unlocked the door, pushed the seat up, and grabbed her duffel bag. She frowned down at the paper cups but said in a jovial mood, "Not today, little friends," then relocked and closed the door and swung the duffel up on her shoulder as she headed into the house.

Once inside she headed straight for the laundry room and threw her smelly workout gear, duffel and all, into the washer and let it do its thing, then immediately started taking her clothes off as she headed through the house, leaving a trail from the living room to her bathroom, where she hopped in the shower. An ex-girlfriend had once commented on this habit. *Not that I mind the show, but you kind of remind me of an out-of-the-park-*

homer that's hit so hard, it sheds layers as it flies. And I'm the outfielder looking for pieces. Sports metaphors had just been how Lisa talked. She was a high school PE teacher and women's softball coach. Lou had gotten used to them and had even found that one kind of sweet.

She was looking forward to dinner with the boys tonight. She didn't really mind that they would be grilling her along with the steaks. She had teased Bill about being a gossip, but she knew their questions came from a good place. Anyway, she had no one else to gush to, not that she was much of a gusher. Her college friends had all scattered to the four winds after graduation, and the friends she'd made since hadn't become as close-knit as her group of irregulars, as they referred to themselves, from college. They had all been geeks and nerds, and once she met them she had felt as if she had found her people.

Now Bill and Dix were her family, and it seemed right that she would talk to them about her date. If her mother had still been alive, she would have asked polite, interested questions and not intruded too much on Lou's privacy. Lou's friends used to tell her how lucky she was to have a mother who cared enough to stay out of her business, and Lou tried to see it from their point of view, but she couldn't always. She sometimes wished her mother would ask her more questions, instead of just asking a few rudimentary ones, almost like she was playing the part of an interested mother but really wasn't. Almost as if she hadn't wanted to get involved.

After her shower, Lou still had several hours before she was due at Bill and Dix's, so after getting dressed in a T-shirt and cargo pants, she pulled the stack of midterm papers out of her satchel and sat down at the kitchen table with a large cup of coffee and a red pen. She used the red pen out of nostalgia mostly, but also conceded that it did stand out better than her favorite black pen did. She'd had a professor in college who had graded with a green pencil and she had never understood why. While the traditional red markup led generations of students to refer to their profs bleeding all over the paper, that green pen had been dubbed ooze.

When she graded, she mostly commented on where a student could have taken their work further and made suggestions on other research they could consult. On *Rate My Professors*, students described her as intense but an easy A, as long as you showed up and did all the things. That was pretty accurate.

Five hours later, after only getting up for more coffee and to check on her laundry, Lou put away the mostly done stack of papers and realized it was time to head over to the boys' place for dinner. She took her cup to the sink and rinsed it, then turned it upside down in the sink. She picked up her keys and phone and turned her phone back on—she often turned it off when she wanted to concentrate on something, whether it was grading, writing, or working out—and saw that she had several email notifications and three texts from Bill, all saying pretty much the same thing: *Where are you?*

She smiled and typed back, *Doing my job. I'm on my way now.* Leaving the phone on vibrate, she put it her pocket and headed for the door.

❖

Dix met Lou at the door and greeted her by putting a kiss on each of her cheeks and handing her a bottle of beer. She accepted the beer and the kisses with a smile and said, "You're only one of two men who are allowed to kiss me."

Bill came in from the living room with his arms open wide and enveloped her in a hug, and said, "As long as I'm the other one." So saying, he kissed her on the left cheek. "How are you, dear?"

She sighed audibly and said, "I have grading fatigue. But other than that, ready for a good medium-rare."

As they made their way into the living room, Dix said, "Why don't you ever insult his cooking?"

Before Lou could respond, Bill jumped in, "Why would she?"

Lou giggled, while Dix stood with his mouth agape. "Guess who's not going to be big spoon tonight?"

"Oh, hush. The last time you spooned me was the night of Maggie's wedding." Bill turned to Lou. "He was feeling frisky after the day's events and attacked me as soon as we got back to our hotel."

"Don't lie to the poor girl." Dix inclined his head to Lou almost conspiratorially and said, "I ask you, do you know any other couple who's been together over twenty years and still has sex as much as we do? Hmm?"

"I don't know how much sex you have." Before either of them could fill her in on this knowledge, she raised a finger of warning. "And I don't want to know. So don't tell me." But she was laughing as she said it.

Bill shrugged and looked at his husband. "She has just been no fun at all today."

"But we love her anyway." Dix smiled and kissed her on the cheek again, then took her by the arm. He said to his husband, "Now go finish up those steaks, while our second-favorite lesbian tells me about her date."

"She is going to tell us together, aren't you, love?"

Lou crossed her arms over her chest and looked at them with fond amusement. "I don't know. I may have to reconsider if I'm your *second*-favorite lesbian."

"I'm sorry, but Maggie was here first," Bill said.

"So you play favorites?"

"Yes, but she's only winning by a hair. After all, she went off and left us, so you are our favorite lesbian left in town."

Lou unclasped her arms and said dryly, "Small compensation."

Dix looked at Bill and said sadly, "Honey, I think we hurt her feelings."

"It can't be helped. It is what it is. I shall return." With that, he turned on his heel and left the living room through the patio door to attend to the grill.

Lou looked out in wonder. "He's actually grilling? Doesn't he know it's October?"

"Oh, honey, that man would grill in the middle of winter. One year he wanted grilled turkey for Thanksgiving and it snowed that year. Didn't matter to him. He was still out there in his heavy winter coat and Cubs hat, you know, the kind with the ball on top?" Dix made a gesture on top of his head to indicate a puffy ball.

"I think they call those beanies now."

Dix *tsk*ed. "It's a hat—a beanie has a propeller on it. Young people would know that if they weren't so stupid."

Lou laughed. "Do you include your students in that?"

"Oh, I include them *especially*. Not really, of course. We all have our own abilities. I love my job, don't get me wrong, but too many students are lured by unscrupulous recruiters who are just trying to fill seats." Dix looked lost in thought for a moment, contemplating his own words.

"That's probably true. Too many kids are pushed to go to college, when they shouldn't."

"I could talk for hours on that topic, so I will force myself not to. Come on and help me set the table."

Lou bowed to him much the same way Steve had bowed to her, in a courtly way, and said, "As you like."

Dix put his hands over his heart and exclaimed, "Be still my heart."

They laughed together as they walked into the kitchen.

❖

Once dinner was served, they all sat around the table enjoying the steaks Bill had prepared and exclaiming over their goodness. She was halfway through her meal before Bill and Dix started asking questions. Bill was first.

"Okay, you've had plenty of food. Tell us."

Before she could, Dix piped up and said, "Sgt. Hottie, reporting for duty."

"I think you're confusing my love life with gay porn."

"You mean it's not?" Bill sounded disappointed.

Lou looked down and pretended to sigh dejectedly. "Alas, it is not. I hope I have not disappointed your expectations of what lesbians are like."

Dix looked at his husband. "I've heard that lesbians can go out and not have sex on the first date."

"What?" Bill sounded shocked.

"It's true," Dix replied.

"He's right." Lou backed him up. "But we make up for it by moving in on the second date."

"Fascinating."

"So when is she moving in?" Dix asked.

Lou shrugged and took a bite of her steak, then said, "Not sure. We haven't set up a second date yet, but I think we will."

"So if you didn't have sex last night, what did you do?"

"What all lesbians do on dates—we had dinner, talked, got to know each other, staged a protest over the unfair wages the waiters were making, then went home." Lou grinned.

Bill looked at Dix. "I hope you're taking notes for our report."

Dix used his fork to pretend to make a note in the air and smiled at Lou.

Bill turned back to Lou. "If you're not going to be honest, you are not getting dessert, missy."

"What's for dessert?"

"Apple cobbler and vanilla ice cream."

Lou considered. "Well…I'll give you more details, but only if it's homemade."

"Is there any other kind?"

"You mean homemade by him or Mrs. Smith?"

"Hush." Bill pointed his finger at Dix and Dix fixed him with a beatific smile and winked at Lou.

"There isn't that much more to tell anyway. After dinner, we went to campus and walked around the duck pond, and then she took me home and kissed me good night."

Bill leaned in. "Was it a good kiss?"

Lou leaned in to Bill. "That depends, is it going in your report?"

"No, this is just between us."

Lou sat up and said wistfully, "It was a very good kiss."

Dix quipped, "It was wrong to compare it to gay porn. That does not sound hot at all."

Lou grinned. "I never said it wasn't hot."

"Finally, some juicy details," Bill said excitedly.

"Nope, that's all you get, mainly because that's all there was."

"And you wonder why Maggie's our favorite."

"Well, if being your favorite means giving you all the intimate details, I guess I'm happy being second best."

"I *knew* there were more details," Dix declared.

"There always are. Don't worry, my dear, we'll get the story out of her yet."

"And my little dog too?"

"You don't have a little dog," Dix said.

"But if you did, yes," Bill declared.

❖

Later that night, when Lou got home, she pulled the midterm papers out and finished grading them, then answered all her emails, most of which were from panicked students. She did what she could to put their fears to rest, then put her laptop and the papers away and went to her room. By the time she called it a night, it was well past midnight, but that was typical. The boys had been disappointed when she didn't stay long after dinner, but she knew she had several more hours of work waiting for her at home.

They had kissed her good-bye at the door and Bill had said, "You will keep us informed, won't you?"

She crossed her heart and said, "I will keep you abreast of everything."

"Oh God, I don't want to be that close to you."

Lou laughed and Dix rolled his eyes.

Sobering, Lou said, "Don't make me give you a bear hug."

"Just go. But let us know what happens."

"Of course."

Now in her room, Lou took off her T-shirt and cargo pants and threw them in a vague direction toward her hamper, and took some joy in flinging her sports bra like the slingshot it was often called in the same direction. There was another T-shirt on her bed, an oversized heather gray one with ARMY STRONG in bold black lettering, that she had taken from her father's closet when he left. It still smelled of his piney scent and was two sizes too big on her, but it was the perfect size to sleep in. She slipped it on and it came to just above her knees. The shoulders fell halfway down her arms. She didn't fill the shirt out the way her father had. The years she had spent learning her craft had given her a lean, toned body, one she was proud of, but not an overly large one. Her shoulders weren't bulging but she did have good definition. And she was okay with that. She hadn't learned her skills for the muscles, but the speed and deftness with which she could now move had come in handy over the years.

She left her bedroom, went into the kitchen, and took a plastic glass from the cabinet above the sink, filled it with iced tea from the fridge, then took it back to her room and set it on her nightstand. She pulled the covers back and settled in, retrieved a paperback novel off the nightstand, and began to read. One of her favorite fantasy writers had recently come out with a new book and she was anxious to read it.

After about a half hour, her phone buzzed on the nightstand. The noise was so loud against the wooden surface and she was so into the book, that she jumped, startled. She chuckled to herself when she realized what she had done. "Bill, I'm going to kill you." But the message wasn't from Bill at all and she smiled. "Oh."

Sorry it's so late, but I just couldn't wait another day. I think etiquette says you're supposed to but I just couldn't. I hope I didn't wake you. If you're just finding this in the morning, good morning. I hope you slept well. If you are reading this in the now, I hope you had a good day today. Whenever you're reading this, I hope you're smiling.

Lou felt her cheeks grow warm and her smile grew. "Oh my God." She typed, *Yes, I'm smiling. Maybe even blushing a little, though I don't know why. Yes, I had a good day. Saw your mother this morning, then did teacher things in the afternoon, then met friends for dinner. How about you?*

Blushing? I'd give anything to see that. But in time, I'm sure. Yes, I saw my mother today too. She was surprisingly polite about not asking me too much. Did she grill you? I hope not.

She was polite to me as well. But she did mention inviting me to dinner and asking for info there. Should I be worried?

Haha. Nah. But I think we should have a second date before I bring you home to Mother.

Well, I've already met your mother, but yes, I agree.

No, you've met Mrs. Adams—you have not met my mother. I assure you, mom mode is much different. I don't know if even your ninja skills will prepare you.

Now I'm worried. So, when and where, soldier?

Are you busy tomorrow night?

You mean go out on a school night? Lol

If you dare.

Okay, I'm game. What time?

Seven? I have something in mind. It's casual attire.

Intrigued. Okay. I'm in.

Good. I'll see you tomorrow night. Good night, Lou.
Good night, Steve.

Lou was about to put the phone back on the nightstand when she remembered her promise to the boys. She texted Bill, *Dr. Lou reporting. Rendezvous scheduled for tomorrow. Not sure what to expect. Will proceed with caution. Please advise.*

The reply came a couple minutes later. *Woman, do you not know what time it is? Some of us need our beauty sleep, though I suppose you wouldn't know anything about that.*

I think that was a compliment.

Mostly. My advice—don't proceed with caution. Go all in and don't hold anything back. Now, good night.

All in? I'm not sleeping with her on the second date just so you can get juicy details.

Did I say that? I just meant, have fun and don't overthink it. Now, go to sleep!

Yes, sir!

You're not hairy enough to call me that.

Giggling, Lou put her phone back on the nightstand. "I don't think I want to know."

Despite Bill's admonition to sleep, she had no intention of doing so. She also couldn't read any longer. Bill knew her well enough to know that overthinking was exactly what she was going to lie there and do, but she couldn't help herself. In spite of the good feelings coursing through her just from texting Steve, her old doubts about dating someone in the military came back to her. It didn't matter that Steve was retired. She had still been in for about ten years, and that much time in could change a person. She knew Steve had seen combat, though it wasn't something she wanted to talk about, and Lou understood that. But it still gave her pause.

She closed her book and put it next to her glass, then took off her glasses and put them on top of the book. Finally she turned off the lamp and settled into the covers. She still didn't sleep but she was in a more comfortable position to overthink things.

CHAPTER SIX

I feel like a rejected Jackson Pollock painting," Lou said with laughter, as she surveyed her clothing and felt her face after their paintball match.

"Why rejected?" Steve asked.

"I don't know about you, but Day-Glo orange and yellow spotted sweats are not something I'd want hanging on my wall." Lou was pulling off pads as she spoke.

"I don't know, I think you look cute." Steve smiled at her and brushed a strand of hair off Lou's face before she kissed her softly.

Lou smiled back. "You have weird taste."

"Not going to argue with that."

"Not even a little?" Lou's smile turned into a grin and it made Steve laugh.

Steve's laughter died down and she caressed the side of Lou's throat and looked at her with concern. "Does it hurt still?"

"Some. Bloody cheap shot." Lou tried to laugh off the pain as she self-consciously rubbed the spot where Steve's hand was. A stray shot from the opposing team had found its way under her gear and hit her on the side of her throat, bringing her to her knees and marking the end of the game for her. Steve had stood in front of her and taken out the shooter while Lou had left the field with her gun raised.

"I never expected the stream of curses that came out of your mouth, though." Steve laughed. "Were some of those Shakespearean insults?"

"Monty Python."

"You are a nerd, aren't you?"

"Geek."

"You bite the heads off chickens?" Steve asked, amused.

"Oh, shut up." Lou put her arms around Steve's neck and kissed her.

"All in all, though, you did very well for someone who doesn't shoot guns for a living."

Lou pulled away and distracted herself with taking off the rest of her gear. "My father taught me."

Steve began to remove her gear as well. "He was into guns?"

"Something like that."

"Oh, that's right, you told me he was in the service."

"Yep."

"So he taught you about guns?"

"And knives and bows and arrows and fighting. He taught me to protect myself." Lou pushed the serious mood she felt coming on aside and forced a smile. "But he didn't teach me how to dodge a bullet, apparently."

Steve grinned again. "Are you talking about me?"

"Only time will tell, soldier, time will tell."

❖

After Steve dropped Lou off at home, she was left feeling almost as if she had inflicted the wound on Lou's neck herself. What had she been thinking, playing paintball on a date? She had had fun right up until the moment she saw Lou drop to her knees. Her first thought was to go to her, but then her soldier side kicked in and she responded accordingly. Besides, she'd had the idea that if she had gone to her side, Lou would have been more upset about that than about the Day-Glo projectile that hit her in the neck. She could already tell that Lou was a determined woman who was more than willing to fight her own battles. The only reason she didn't fire back at her attacker was respect for the rules of the field.

Even so, guilt aside, Steve had been impressed with Lou's ability to just walk it off. She hated to admit it, but she had found Lou's perseverance kind of sexy. She had always liked a woman who could hold her own in any situation. It was a quality Cairyn had lacked, though it was uncharitable to think that way. That didn't make it any less true. Cairyn's mother had depended on her husband for everything and had taught her daughter to expect the same. Cairyn could cook and clean and manage the house, but she found it hard to follow a budget or hold down a job. She had finally admitted to Steve one night, after she had lost yet another job, that her mother hadn't raised her to work for a living. She was expected to marry well and live off her spouse's income. When Cairyn had come out to her family, her mother's major concern had been Cairyn's financial state, and she worried Cairyn wouldn't find anyone to take care of her.

When they became a couple, Steve told Cairyn that that would have to change. As an enlisted soldier, she didn't make much and wasn't likely to unless she rose in the ranks to officer. But instead of trying to hold down a job, Cairyn pushed Steve to raise in rank instead, not realizing that would mean Steve would be away from home more.

Steve pushed aside thoughts of Cairyn after she gave the necklace a quick, perfunctory kiss before she reached her house. Lou was different than Cairyn, much different. Lou didn't need anyone, and Steve admired her strength.

❖

"Who plays paintball on a date? That's like a messy game of tag for grownups." Bill sounded scandalized as Lou sat on their couch telling them about her date with Steve the night before.

"Julia Stiles did with Heath Ledger. It looked like fun." Dix smiled at Lou and she laughed.

"It was fun."

"Don't encourage his pop culture references—you'll make him insufferable."

Dix tapped Bill on the shoulder and asked, "Why don't we ever do fun things like that when we go out?"

Bill turned to look at his husband. "What's wrong with you?"

"You mean it doesn't appeal to your theatrical side?" Dix asked.

"Need I remind you, I'm in costume design? All that reminds me of is dirty costumes. And those things aren't cheap."

"It usually washes out," Lou said between giggles.

Bill rolled his eyes. "And what about the chance for injury? I can't believe she took you someplace where you got hurt." Bill gently rubbed his thumb over the bruise that had formed on Lou's neck and clucked his tongue in disgust.

Lou turned her head slightly so that he could see the bruise and tried not to wince as his thumb found the sorest spot. She turned back around and forced a smile. "It was a lucky shot! It wasn't Steve's fault. Plus, she slaughtered the bastard who got me. Never piss off a soldier when she's holding a gun."

Dix sniggered and Bill finally smiled. "Well, at least you found your very own knight in shining armor."

Lou looked affronted. "I don't need a knight in shining armor. I can take care of myself. I would have done the same for her."

"Oh, love, it is okay to let someone take care of you from time to time. You don't always have to walk it off." Bill's eyes were full of concern now, as he took her hand.

Lou leveled her gaze at him. "Bill, I love you dearly, but I have to tell you, you look nothing like Oprah and I am not about to break down. But I appreciate your concern." She removed her hand from his and patted him on the cheek, then placed a small kiss where her hand had been.

"Of course I'm not Oprah—I'm a broke college professor who can barely afford *my* favorite things, let alone hers. And I don't want you to cry, love, not unless you need to."

"It doesn't hurt anymore. It's just a bruise—I've had worse." Lou shrugged.

"So you say."

"I do say." Lou quickly stood up from the couch and declared, "Weren't we going out to Homer's for dinner? Or did you lure me over here under false pretenses?"

Dix stood and held out his arm, and Lou put her hand on his arm and smiled. "A gentleman never disappoints a lady." Dix looked behind him to Bill and asked, "Are you coming?"

Bill stood and took Dix's other arm. "Of course, but I have to ask...how are you planning to skip down that yellow brick road when we can't fit through the door like this?"

Dix smiled at Bill and placed a small kiss on his lips. "Magic, my dear, magic."

"Well, will one of you click your heels together? I'm starving."

Dix did so and said, "There's no place like Homer's, there's no place like Homer's."

Lou laughed and Bill said, "That didn't work. Let's try the door this time."

Dix turned to Lou and said, "Some people just don't believe in the power of magic."

Lou smiled. "But some of us do."

Chapter Seven

The only thing Lou hated about the bruise was that she had to work the next day. By Tuesday morning, the bruise had turned a nice dark purple and there was a knot in the center of it that was still tender. Several of her students looked at her in shock, and she chuckled and said, "You should see the other guy."

Melissa, a small redhead in the front row, looked the most alarmed. "Did you really get into a fight, Dr. Silver?"

Lou smiled at her. "Yes and no. I played paintball yesterday and a lucky shot found its way under my helmet. Let that be a lessen to you...never let yourself be so complacent that you think you're not going to get hurt if you are fighting, in any type of fighting. Odds say you will get hurt, but it doesn't have to be a blow that takes you out of the fight, not if you know how to protect yourself." She went on from there, using the incident as a teachable moment. Learning how to fight safely was key to all combat-related activities, and that especially included stage combat. She had always taught the two main rules of stage combat: make it look real and don't get hurt. She usually excelled at both of those things, in and out of combat situations.

When class was over, she deflected more questions about the paintball incident, but she was touched at their concern.

As she was leaving her classroom, Charles walked up to her with a look of concern that turned into a mild expression of shock, and he stopped in his tracks a few feet from her. "Wow, when Judy said you had a large bruise, she wasn't kidding. Are you all right?"

Lou smiled to reassure him and walked closer. "I'm fine. It was just a stray paint ball."

"Looks rather nasty. Does it hurt?"

"Not anymore," she lied. "It looks worse than it is."

"Well, I'm surprised you came into the classroom like that."

Lou wasn't sure, but she thought she heard a bit of reproach in his voice, an unspoken admonishment. She shrugged it off. "What was I going to do? Stay home because of a bruise? Besides, in my line of work, bruises are common."

"Yes, well, there are often prospective student tours walking through the building…" He trailed off but he didn't have to finish.

"I will go hide in my office, Charles, lest a parent or donor sees me and wonders just what kind of school we're running here." She chuffed him on the shoulder with a smile and it made her think of Rachel and how much she'd treated Charles with irreverence. She had to bite back the chuckle she felt was imminent, reminding herself that he was her boss.

Charles looked at his arm where she had playfully punched him and frowned. "Yes, well, you know what I mean."

"I know exactly what you mean, Charles. Is that all?"

"What? Oh, yes. Sorry, that was all." He stood aside and she walked past him.

Inside, she was fighting back her anger and impatience at him. He wasn't a bad boss for the most part, but his constant insistence on keeping up appearances was exhausting and chafed a bit. As she set her class materials on her desk, she said softly, "Maggie Parks, I totally understand you." She sighed as she sat in her chair. Not that she was thinking of leaving, as Maggie Parks had done in the face of departmental hostility, but she could understand the impulse to do so. When she took this job, she had told herself that she was going to stop running and that it was time to settle down and put down roots. She could tolerate Charles because she understood him. She knew what motivated him. She knew that if she did her job to the best of her ability and didn't draw attention to herself, then Charles would be happy. She had no intention of drawing attention to herself. That was the last thing she wanted.

❖

Lou and Steve were sitting on what had become their sofa in Lou's favorite café. It'd only been a couple of weeks since they had started dating and they were enjoying finding things out about each other.

"So, I know you're a ninja"—Lou chuckled at Steve's words—"and a badass, but I don't really know what you do over there." Steve gestured vaguely behind her, out the windows. The campus was just a few blocks in that direction. "I mean, I know what you teach, but what's your passion?" Steve grinned and raised an eyebrow.

Lou laughed and asked, "Are you asking about my research interests?"

"Yes."

"Are you sure you want to know? I mean, it can be really dull if it's not your thing."

"How bad could it be?"

"Let me put it this way—one of my old college friends is a bio professor in Pennsylvania. She recently told me her research has something to do with lizards and spatial memory. I didn't understand the half of it." Lou laughed.

"Well, considering what you teach, I'm sure it's way more interesting and doesn't involve lizards. So, what *are* you researching?"

With a straight face, Lou said, "Medieval lizard knights and their epic battles." She held the face for a few seconds, long enough for Steve to realize she was joking, then she burst out laughing.

"For a second I was picturing it."

"You know, it would be cool, wouldn't it?"

"Totally. Little lizard swords..."

"I can just see a gecko riding on the back of a Komodo dragon for the jousting bits." They broke up in laughter.

Steve picked up her stirring stick and held it out like a sword. "I'm here to avenge my father, prepare to meet your doom!"

In response, Lou picked up her stirrer as well, and said, "Your father smelled like goats anyway, no great loss."

They laughed together as they broke out into a mock duel. They didn't care that other diners were looking their way. They were having too much fun. The duel ended when Steve's stick broke and she looked at it in despair.

Lou raised her fist triumphantly and declared, "Yes! Victory is mine! Better luck next time, soldier." Then she smiled and planted a small kiss on Steve's lips.

"If that's your spoils of war I'll lose to you any day."

"We're not at war, Sergeant, but I'll let you know if that changes." Lou smiled coyly at her over her coffee cup.

"Good. I like to keep informed of these things." Steve lightly poked Lou on the knee with her broken stick. "So besides fighting lizards, what else are you studying?"

"You really want to know?"

"Yeah."

Lou took a deep breath and then said, "My current research project is a book entitled *Playing Chess with Fortuna: Sir Gawain and the Loyal Knight Errant on Stage*." Lou shrugged and looked somewhat sheepish. "Because academic titles are nothing without a colon."

"Don't downplay it—it sounds kinda fascinating."

"You don't have to say that. I'll still date you." Lou grinned.

"No, I mean it. I'm impressed and intrigued. What's your ultimate goal with this research?"

With a wry expression, Lou replied, "Tenure."

Steve laughed appreciatively. "Knight errant, huh? So you're a romantic?"

"I don't know that I'd say that, but I do believe in chivalry. And you do too."

Steve blushed. "I believe in manners. My mother taught me well."

"No, it's more than that. And I'm not complaining." Lou touched Steve's face tenderly and gave her a smile. They were sharing this sweet moment when the door to the café opened, which Lou ignored.

Then a disgusted sounding female voice called out, "Ugh, I can't believe my teacher is looking all gooey-eyed like that. Never thought I'd see the day."

Steve looked like she was about to defend Lou, but her dark look turned to surprise when Lou laughed and said, "I'm not your teacher anymore, Rachel. Hello, Bobby."

"You will always be my teacher, Sifu." Rachel stood off to the side of the sofa Lou and Steve sat on, Bobby at her side, and bowed.

Lou inclined her head in kind, then stood and hugged them both, then introduced them to Steve. The newcomers pulled up chairs. "How'd you know I was here, and why didn't you tell me you were coming today? I thought it was next week for Thanksgiving?"

"Please, stalking you wouldn't be hard. You go like three places: campus, the ninja gym thingy, and here. It wasn't even an educated guess, really."

Lou smiled. "I go other places. And to my second question?"

Rachel sighed. "It was going to be next week, but at the last minute, my parents changed it to this week so they can go on some cruise. The only upside is now we won't have to do two Thanksgivings in one day."

Bobby grinned and rubbed his stomach. "Just as long as I still get two Thanksgivings, doesn't bother me."

Rachel smacked his knee playfully, and rolled her eyes for Lou's and Steve's benefits. "Walking tapeworm, I swear."

Bobby began rubbing the spot she had smacked and said,

"That was my bad leg, you know?" But he could barely suppress his grin.

Rachel looked at him and said, "No it's not. I was there, remember? Bedside vigil, and all that? Oh, what do you know? You spent most of that time in a coma."

"One day! I spent one day unconscious. I would hardly call that a coma. At least you didn't go all Shirley MacLaine at my bedside and start screaming for my meds." Bobby grinned and Rachel rolled her eyes again. Lou and Steve were laughing at them.

Rachel turned back to Lou, ignoring Bobby. "So now that we're here, we going to get out of here and go out for dinner, or what?" She looked between Lou and Steve.

Lou looked at Steve as well. "I know we haven't discussed dinner yet, but you want to?"

"Alas, I cannot. I forgot to tell you earlier, but Mom signed us both up for this cooking class and I have to go. I'm sorry. But it was lovely meeting you two." Steve smiled at Rachel and Bobby.

Rachel waved her hand dismissively. "Of course it was."

Steve laughed as she stood and Lou stood with her. "I will see you later, my dear." Steve gave Lou a chaste kiss on the cheek.

"Call me later and tell me how class went."

"I will." With one final smile and wave, Steve was gone.

Rachel, who had turned to watch Steve leave, addressed her comment to Lou. "I'm sure you hate to see her go, but mm, to watch her leave," she said wistfully.

"Hello? I'm right here, you know?" Bobby said.

"Yeah, so am I," Lou said. "But you're not wrong." Lou craned her neck to catch a glimpse of Steve through the windows as she walked to her car.

Rachel turned and faced her teacher again and raised her hand in the air. "Way to go, teach, good job." Lou met Rachel's high five with enthusiasm.

"Still here," Bobby said, somewhat dejectedly.

Rachel turned to him and grabbed his chin. "I know, my love, and you're cute too." She gave him a small peck on the lips and Lou sat back smiling, delighting in their company.

❖

After a while, Bobby left to go meet his brother, and then it was just Rachel and Lou sitting next to each other on the sofa. Rachel grinned and smacked Lou on the knee. "So, are you going to tell me about that hot piece who kissed you or not?" Rachel's eyes danced in mischief and it was hard not to get caught up in her spirit.

Lou looked at her somewhat dubiously. "Hot piece? Is that any way to talk to the teacher you purport to respect?" Lou tried to look stern and was able to for a couple of seconds.

Rachel waved her hand in the air in a dismissive gesture. "Oh, I'll respect you in the morning. That's then. Gossip now, woman!"

"You appear to be living vicariously through me. Maybe we should talk about that," Lou said calmly, fighting a grin of her own.

"Why would I have to do that, when I have my own hot piece? You've met him."

"So things are still going well between you? How's his recovery been? I noticed a slight limp when he walked in."

Rachel turned serious. "Yeah, the cold weather really does bother him. I wasn't thinking about that when I asked him to move to Minnesota. But he's doing well otherwise. He doesn't limp all the time, only when the weather gets to him. He gets migraines sometimes too. Par for the course, they say. But he's not letting it stop him. He's loving grad school and still finds time for his music." The serious look passed and she grinned again and pointed an accusing finger at Lou. "Ah, I see what you did there. You're not getting out of this conversation. Tell me about

Steve. She's really hot." Rachel nodded her head as if agreeing to a question that hadn't been asked.

"Yes, so you've said." Lou pointed her own accusing finger at Rachel and said, "Hands off, she's mine," then laughed.

Rachel put her right hand in the air and said, "I solemnly swear not to steal your babe. I have my own."

Lou sighed, as if put upon. "Okay, then. What can I tell you? She's retired military, has courtly manners, she makes me laugh and blush. And, as you've noticed, looks good in pants that show off her…assets." Lou grinned.

"Look at you, doing pretty well for yourself. Well, I'm glad you found someone to appreciate you. Wait, what about your geek side? Does she know about that?" Rachel looked worried for a moment, but it just made Lou laugh.

"She's beginning to. She has her own geek side. She collects comic books, for one thing."

"Get out! Like superhero comic books? Who's her favorite?"

"Not superhero, no. Lesbian comic books."

"There is such a thing?"

"Rachel, I will smack you off this sofa if you tell me you've never heard of *Dykes to Watch Out For* or *Jane's World*."

Rachel looked at her blankly and shook her head. "Nope, sorry. Before my time, I guess." Rachel grinned mischievously.

Lou pulled her hand back as if to strike her and Rachel put her arm up to block. "I learned something from my sifu."

Lou inclined her head. "So you did. But that doesn't excuse your not knowing those comics. They are iconic and you will show some respect. I'll send you some for Christmas."

"Fine. Anyway, back to business. So you're both geeks who are into hitting things, and she has perfect manners and looks good in tight pants. I think I'm caught up."

"Good. And you're working in theater, your young man is back in school and on the road to recovery, and it's cold in Minnesota. I think I'm caught up too." Lou smiled.

"Yep." They were silent a moment, then Rachel asked, "So what's really going on?"

"I was about to ask you the same question."

Rachel sighed. "Just, same ol', same ol'. You know?" She raised one shoulder, trying to make whatever was on her mind seem like no big deal.

"Having doubts again?"

"Well, not really, I mean…not so much. It's just that…sorry, hard to find words for it."

"I understand."

"I mean, I love him, there's no question, but did you see his face?"

"Yes, I saw the stubble."

"And it's like that everywhere! And I mean, everywhere." As if realizing her voice had started to rise, Rachel spoke more softly. "Been thinking of asking if he'll wax his back. Would that be selfish?"

"I think that's a fine line. But is that what's really bothering you—his hair?"

"The other day, I was talking to one of the actresses in the company and she asked me how many boyfriends I've had. I'd told her he's the only one. She thought I meant we had been high school sweethearts. I told her, no, I'm a lesbian. Then, she was all, So, are you one of those lesbians who sleep with men or something? And I said, No, I'm the lesbian who sleeps with Bobby."

Lou laughed. "Sorry, go on."

"I just…I feel like I have to declare my lesbian status all the time. Like I should start wearing pride rings and dressing more like Rory, or something. I mean, it's not like I didn't expect this, it's just…It's difficult, you know?" Rachel put her arm on the back of the couch and rested her head on her hand.

"I know. Identity is important. Have you talked to him about this?"

"Some. I don't want him to think I don't love him, you know? I do. I just don't want to lose me in the process."

Lou put her hand on Rachel's knee and nodded in understanding. "Remember what we talked about before? That it matters less what people think of you, and more what you think of yourself? You know who you are. If sometimes you have to declare that to people, fine. But the main thing is that you stay true to who you are and don't conform to what you think other people expect of you." They shared a soft look, then Lou sat back and said, "But maybe a labrys tattoo wouldn't hurt."

Rachel laughed. "Oh, yeah, I'm so the tattoo type."

"People definitely wouldn't expect it of you."

"You got a point there." Rachel jumped a little and looked, annoyed, toward her pants pocket. "Hold on." She pulled out her phone and read the message, then sighed. "Looks like it's time to feed the boy's tapeworm. He's starting to whine. Want to come with?"

"Ah, thank you, but I will have to decline. I have to go home and do all the things. You two have fun, and we will definitely have to all get together before you leave."

"Definitely. I do get a hug, right?"

"Of course." They stood and Lou hugged her good-bye, then walked her out to her car. They waved, then Lou drove home.

❖

When Steve left the café, it wasn't to go to a cooking class with her mother. She went home, chastising herself the whole way for lying to Lou. Not only shouldn't she have done so, but it was a bad lie, easily discovered. Lou would see her mother on the weekend and she could easily ask how the cooking class was going. Steve smacked the steering wheel and muttered, "Dammit, you suck at lying."

She wasn't even sure why she felt the need to run out of the café like that, but she suddenly felt an urgent need to leave when Rachel and Bobby showed up. Not that it had anything to do with them, exactly. It was just that suddenly, it seemed like the world was going too fast and she was caught up in something that was spinning her around, and she needed to get off the ride. Maybe it was the domesticity of the situation, how natural it seemed that they were in a relationship. But it was moving too fast for Steve.

As she sat on the sofa, she could feel her heart start to beat faster and her face felt hot. The noises in the room had started to blend together and the voices were becoming indistinct. At the time, she knew what all those things meant and knew she needed to get out of the situation. After hugging Lou good-bye, she'd practically run back to her car, barely remembering to put her seat belt on. She could feel their eyes on her. She worried they could tell what was happening, but she tried to tell herself that was ridiculous. She'd been having panic attacks for several years, and by now she had developed methods to deal with them in such a way that others didn't even notice she was having them. But that didn't stop her from worrying that Lou noticed and might think less of her, that she was crazy or something. Before she put the car in drive, she took a deep breath—once, twice, three times—then brought the Capricorn pendant up to her lips and kissed it. Then she felt she could leave.

A few minutes later, she pulled into her driveway and turned off the ignition, then put her head on her folded arms resting on the steering wheel and exhaled. *I'm fine. It's okay. I'm fine.* After a moment, she sat back up, took the keys out of the car, and opened the car door. She chuckled to herself when she realized she almost forgot to unbuckle the seat belt, the one she had almost forgotten to buckle in the first place. She pushed the release button and got out of the car and somehow made it to her front door. When she got inside, she threw her keys into a two-toned blue ceramic ashtray on a table by the door that had a small Meramec Caverns decal in the bottom of it. It had never been used as an ashtray, as no one in her family smoked. She had taken it with her when she left as a reminder of home. Her keys hit the bottom with a clank, and then she kicked off her shoes at the door and set them neatly in the boot tray.

Steve walked across her neatly kept living room to the hallway that led to her bedroom. Once there, she went to her dresser and pulled out a T-shirt and nylon shorts, then changed into them, making sure to put the clothes she just took off in the hamper in the corner. Then she retrieved a pair of tennis shoes from the closet and left the room, walking back through the house to the door in the kitchen that led out into the garage.

This room was not a place for her car. This was her gym. In one corner, there was a weight bench and bar behind it. On another wall were the free weights. Bikes hung off one wall, one for city riding and one for off-road, and on another wall hung jump ropes and boxing gloves. The heavy bag hung in the center of the room. And that's where she went, after she put on the gloves.

She stood there for quite a while, she wasn't sure how long, punching the bag. Long enough to work up a sweat, which she didn't notice until it reached her eyes. She wiped it away with the back of her arm and kept going. Finally, out of breath, she stopped and tore off her gloves and hung them back on the peg on the wall. She turned around and looked at the room, at her equipment, wiped more sweat off her forehead and said to herself, "I miss this." Chuckling to herself, she pulled the pendant out from under her shirt and brought it to her lips with a small smile and kissed it, then tucked it back in and went into the house to shower.

❖

Lou left the café and headed home. Once inside, she kicked off her shoes near the sofa and threw her keys on her table, not bothering to pick them up when they slid to the floor. She went to the fridge to retrieve a bottle of water, then opened her laptop, which she had left on the table, and typed in her password. She pulled up the novel draft with a sigh. "No rest for the weary." She was trying to get back into the story she'd been neglecting for the last several weeks, but the muse, that fickle bitch, wasn't showing up. She opened her music streaming app and asked it to play her favorite musical style, rockabilly, then returned to her writing. A Stray Cats song immediately started to play, but not one she was familiar with. She couldn't get into it and it was making her more frustrated. She skipped that song. It changed to a Chuck Berry one instead. Better, but it still wasn't doing anything for her. "Rock Around the Clock" came on and she smiled. "Oh, hell yeah!"

Instead of writing, Lou stood up from her chair and started dancing around her kitchen, singing along. When that song was over, an Elvis song came on: "Fever." She smiled to herself and started to snap her fingers in time to the music, moving slowly and sensually, with her eyes closed. The song changed to "Can't Help Falling in Love," and Lou stopped dancing, but the smile stayed in place. Then she shook her head. "No, stop that. Stop thinking that way. Elvis, I don't need this right now." She skipped that song too, though skipping Elvis seemed like sacrilege. "Yakety Yak" played next, and she started dancing again. She was startled by her phone buzzing in her pocket, and yelped. Laughing at herself, she pulled it out and saw that Bill was calling.

"Hello. Just let me turn the music down." She reached over to her laptop and paused the music. "Okay, what's up?"

"Why are you out of breath? Were you muse dancing again?"

Lou laughed. "I told you about that?" Lou resumed her chair and took a drink of her water.

"Don't you tell me everything?"

"No, just most things. Besides, I have to get that bitch here somehow."

"What bitch?"

"The muse! Try to keep up."

"Honey, if this is how you talk about her, no wonder she's

not showing up. You need to romance her and say nice things to her. Make her want you."

"Bill, you do know she's not real, right?"

"Bite your tongue. You've just cursed yourself—I hope you know that."

"I think I've already done that a long time ago. It seems like she's taken a powder on this story. Also, I'm a little disturbed about how you describe my relationship with her. I don't want to seduce my muse. That's just creepy." Lou sat back in her chair and stretched her legs out in front of her. When she did so, she felt something under her foot and looked under the table to see her keys on the floor. She dragged them closer with her foot, then reached down and picked them back up and put them next to her on the table.

"Anything's gotta be better than you dancing around your living room to old rock and roll songs. I mean, how does that work, exactly? You just shimmy those boyish hips of yours and hope she'll be enticed by that?"

"Boyish hips? What do you mean, boyish hips? I don't have boyish hips." Lou twisted around in the chair to try to see what he was talking about.

"That's what you get caught up on? Anyway, I didn't call to talk about your boyish hips, or your bad lesbian dancing—"

Lou interrupted him. "Why is my dancing bad *lesbian* dancing? And who said it was bad? You've never seen it—you're just assuming." She grinned, though he couldn't see.

"How could it not be, with those hips? But I digress."

"Hey…"

"As I said, I digress. I was just calling to invite you and your young paramour over for dinner, or a friendly game of Parcheesi, you know, as people do."

"Parcheesi? What, are you eighty? And why do I hear Admiral Ackbar screaming in my head right now? Hmm?"

"That's that guy from *Star Trek*, right?"

"Wars! *Star Wars.* Seriously?"

"Hey, I can't keep up with all that geeky shit. I have a life."

"Why are you being such a bitch today? First, I have boyish lesbian hips that can't dance, then you throw my favorite fandom under the bus, and me along with it. What's wrong with you?" Lou was still smiling, but she was also concerned about him. Bill didn't talk much with her about personal things, but she wanted him to know she was there if he needed her.

Bill sighed. "It's nothing. Just one of those days. Sorry, love. But the invitation was sincere. We would like to get to know the one who has stolen your heart. It's tradition for all the lesbians we know. We must approve their dates."

Lou chuckled. "What, two lesbian friends, and suddenly it's a tradition?"

"A tradition has to start somewhere. So, are you game?"

"I got a bad feeling…"

"Oh, stop it. Just ask your nerf herder and get back to me."

"Oh, a correct reference. I'm so proud of you." Lou chuckled.

"Oh, shut up." They ended the call with laughter.

Elvis's "A Little Less Conversation" started to play and Lou smacked her hands together. "All right, you Greek bitch, let's get some work done." She put her fingers on the keyboard and began to type.

CHAPTER EIGHT

Steve was just getting out of the shower when she heard her mother's voice coming from her living room.

"Where are you, Stephanie? I know you're here—I saw your car in the driveway."

Steve grabbed her towel off the towel rack, quickly wiped her face, and hollered out, "Just getting out of the shower. Give me a minute." She dried her hair, then the rest of her body, then hung the towel back on the rack. Next, she donned her clothes that were piled neatly on the counter, a clean T-shirt and a pair of sweats with ARMY written down the leg in black letters. A quick look in the steamed-over mirror, where she had wiped a spot clean, reminded her to run her hands through her close-cropped hair. There, it looked fine. Then she opened the bathroom door to go face her mother.

She found her in the kitchen, staring intently into Steve's refrigerator. Steve smiled. "Looking for the meaning of life? Why so serious?"

Her mother turned to her. "No, I'm looking for something edible to eat. Do you never cook at home?" Steve started to speak, but her mother cut her off. "I mean, something besides frozen pizzas and those freeze-dried noodles you used to eat in college."

"Yes, I cook things other than those. Just last Sunday I made you that great noodle dish, remember?" Steve took her own look in the fridge and came out with a beer.

"No, my love child, you didn't. That came out of the freezer, premade. You think I didn't see that?"

Steve took a swig of her beer, then looked at her mother, amused. "Love child? I don't think you're using that term correctly."

Her mother popped her lightly on the back of the head. "Of course I am. Don't correct your mother. It was the seventies, your father and I weren't married yet…What would you call it?" After rooting around in Steve's fridge, she pulled out bacon and a carton of eggs. "I saw on your shelf that you have spaghetti. I'll make you my fabulous carbonara, even if you don't have all the right cheeses. It'll still be wonderful." She took her items to the counter, then said over her shoulder, "Can you get me the parmesan?"

Steve grabbed it for her, then asked, "Can we go back to this love child thing? You never told me this."

"I didn't think you were old enough to handle it, but you're over forty now. Should I have waited until you were fifty?" She busied herself making food, with her back to Steve.

"I'm just surprised, is all. I didn't know you and Dad were hippies. Please tell me there are pictures somewhere."

"Well, I wouldn't say we were hippies—that was mostly over by the time you were born. We never looked the part, but some of our friends…Well, anyway, would you rather I call you my bastard child?" Her mother turned around with a twinkle in her eye and grinned, then went back to the sink and put water in a pot.

Smiling into her beer, Steve said, "No, I would not like that much at all."

"I didn't think so."

"So, wait, did you guys do drugs?"

She shut off the water, carried it over to the stove and placed it on a burner, then turned up the flame. "It always amuses me when children find out their parents had lives before they came along. Almost as if the world was on hold, waiting for them to be born." She turned around to grab a skillet from inside the oven. "Really, you should find a better place for these."

"I'll look into it. You never really answered my question, you know?"

"I didn't?" Steve shook her head. "Oh. Well, hand me the bacon, would you?" Steve handed it to her. "Thank you, love."

"You're not going to, are you?"

"My sources say no."

"Great, now my mother's a Magic 8-Ball. What's next, lava lamps and hookah pipes?"

Nonchalantly, her mother replied, "Well, a girl's gotta have a hobby."

Steve laughed, then kissed her mother on the cheek. "I love you. You're awesome."

Her mother blushed but came back with, "Yes, well, I'm glad you realize that. Speaking of awesome people—"

"Here we go." Steve didn't give her mother a chance to continue. "I was wondering when you would ask me. You've been rather quiet about this up until now."

"What? What am I going to ask you, Miss Know-It-All?"

Steve got a mixing bowl down from a shelf and started to crack the eggs into it without being asked. "You want to ask me about Lou. You've been restraining yourself up till now. Quite frankly, I'm surprised you haven't given yourself a coronary or something."

"Bite your tongue. Don't say words like that to someone my age. I need to buy you some wooden spoons so I can spank you with them."

Steve lightly smacked her butt. "Buns of steel. Wouldn't do any good. Nice try, though." Setting the bowl aside, she said, "Your eggs are done."

"Thank you, sweets. Now, who said I was going to ask about Lou? But since you brought her up…"

Steve narrowed her eyes. "Mother…"

"Oh, don't act like it's a surprise. As you say, I've been restraining myself up until now. Just tell me, do you think this relationship has potential?"

"Potential for what?"

"Don't act so coy. You know, to last? As far as I know, you haven't dated anyone since Cairyn. At least, not more than once. I was beginning to worry."

"I wasn't ready."

"I know. I didn't mean you should have been in a hurry. No one has the right to tell you how long to grieve, not even your mother. I just worried that you would get lost in it, that's all."

"I think I was, for a while. But it's getting better. I like Lou a lot. I think it does have potential." A smile played at her lips and she felt a blush rising. She hid her face as much as she could by taking a sip of her beer.

"Good. Just tell me when I can ask for a family discount." Her mother's eyes danced with mischief.

"Mother, I am not dating her so you can get a discount on kung fu lessons."

"Then why are you dating her?"

"You've met her—she's awesome."

"Well, I know she's a great teacher, but I don't know much about her otherwise. When are you going to invite us both to dinner? Don't you think it's time?"

"And scare her off? I thought you wanted this relationship to work."

"Very funny, young lady. I think it's time I got to know her as my daughter's girlfriend, and not just as my sifu." She pointed a finger in Steve's face. "Make it happen."

Steve sighed. "Fine. I'll see what I can do." Steve returned the gesture. "Just behave. No embarrassing questions. Or embarrassing pictures."

"Well, that rather limits what I can talk about, then. I guess I'll have to think of other things. But you can't stop me from bringing out the embarrassing photos—that's my right and privilege. It's in the Bill of Rights."

"I don't remember that from social studies class."

"I meant the Mom's Bill of Rights. You would know that if you'd given me a grandchild."

"Oh, jeez."

"Getting to bring up not having grandchildren is in there too, along with guilt about not calling enough. Which you cleverly got to sidestep by being in the military and not always being able to. But you're back on civvy ground now and you will do as I say." She arched an eyebrow at Steve and tried to look serious.

Steve stood at attention and brought her right hand up to her forehead. "Yes, Drill Sergeant!" But she couldn't suppress the grin.

"Damn right! At ease, soldier, and get me a whisk."

Steve did as told.

❖

Later that evening, after her mother left, Steve sent Lou a text. She had gotten in the habit of texting instead of calling because she knew Lou was always busy, and she didn't want to presume that she always had the time to sit and talk, even though she would much rather have talked to Lou instead.

Hello, sweetness, just wanted to tell you that my mother has finally gotten around to saying she wants to have dinner together. I convinced her to do the cooking. Are you free next weekend?

Lou replied, *Oh, what a coincidence! Bill wants to do the same thing. I'm sure for the same reasons. They were thinking Friday, what day was your mother thinking?*

Sunday. She said, If she's not sick of me by then. I think she means because of the lesson earlier in the day.

Right. On the mat it's all business, so there won't be any problems. Besides, don't tell her I said this, but she's my favorite student. Unless you think it would win me points.

Steve chuckled. *My mother adores you, your points couldn't go any higher.*

Good to know. See you Friday, soldier.

Steve thought the smile would be permanently affixed to her face.

Chapter Nine

On Tuesday afternoon, Lou decided she needed a little time in the gym by herself. It'd already been a long week, and it was only Tuesday. On Monday, Charles had called a staff meeting that seemed to go on for hours. She hadn't even paid attention to most of it. She just sat doodling on the notepad she had brought with her, hoping it looked as if she was taking notes. Then three students had come up to her asking for extensions on their final papers due in two weeks. None of them had sufficient reason for an extension. She had fixed each of them with her steely-eyed glare and denied their requests.

One student had started to protest that he had three other papers to write, hoping that would earn him sympathy. Again, she didn't budge. "You're in grad school. It goes with the territory. I don't mean to sound unsympathetic, but this is what you signed up for."

The semester would be over in less than a month and she would welcome the break. In the meantime, she needed to have some time sweating for her own sake. Maybe do some strength and endurance training, which she had been neglecting as of late. She needed to clear her head, and there was nowhere better to do that than the gym. She walked through the main room, past the mats where the kung fu training was held, and into the back room where the actual gym was. The Wushuguan offered other services, besides kung fu for all ages. They also offered kickboxing classes, a weight-loss boot camp, self-defense instruction, and personal training. Sometimes the gym was crowded, but Tuesday afternoons were usually pretty open. Besides Lou, there were just a couple of guys lifting weights as a team, and a few people on treadmills. Lou went to the universal gym in the back first to do a warm-up with some of the cable exercises there.

She set her water bottle on the floor near the machine, then went over to the rack on the wall and grabbed an odd-looking contraption, with a padded hand grip and a cloth strap that formed a triangle, at the end of which dangled a D ring. She used the ring to attach it to the pulley, then adjusted the weight to thirty-five pounds. Then she adjusted her stance and began to do bicep curls with her right hand, doing three sets of fifteen for one arm, then switching arms and doing a high set of twenty reps. Once those were done, she switched out the strap for a tricep rope, which was just a fancy name for a piece of rope with hard plastic ball-shaped grips on the ends and a metal attachment in the middle to clip it to the pulley. She left the weight where it was and went on with her exercises. She paused between sets for drinks of water, making sure to stay hydrated.

As she rounded the side of the universal to do the lat pull down, she could see the door of the gym from where she sat. She saw her sifu, Sifu Ann, showing a new person around the gym. Instead of sitting down and continuing with her exercises, she watched as Steve was given a tour, not sure what to make of it. Before she could process the sight of Steve in her place, they were upon her and Steve was smiling at her.

"Hey." Steve smiled and gave her a small wave.

She was confused but gave Steve a perfunctory smile. "Hello."

Ann looked from one to the other. "You two know each other?"

Before Lou could answer, Steve replied, "Yep. She's kinda my girlfriend."

Ann looked surprised. "Oh, I wasn't aware. Well, I'll leave

you to it, then. If you have any more questions, you can ask me…
or Lou, I guess. Welcome." She smiled, then walked away.

Lou stood up and grabbed the lat bar, and after adjusting the
weight, she sat down to do her reps. She didn't say anything to
Steve, who watched her in silence. When the set was done, Lou
stood again and gently let go of the bar, then grabbed her water
bottle from the floor next to her and took a drink.

Finally, Steve asked, "Are you mad at me?"

Lou briefly glanced at her as she stood up and grabbed the
bar again. Before she started her second set, she asked, "No,
why?"

Steve shrugged. "I don't know, just seems like you're upset.
I mean, maybe I shouldn't take it personally, maybe you've
just had a bad day, or you're just trying to concentrate on your
workout. I get that. I just can't help wondering, you know?"
Steve shrugged one shoulder again and looked a little sheepish.

Lou stood up again after finishing her second of three sets,
then resumed her seat and looked up at Steve. "Yes, it's been a
long week already."

Steve leaned against the machine and fixed Lou with a
concerned look. "You want to talk about it?"

Standing up to grab the bar for her last set, Lou replied, "Not
really."

"Okay. I should probably get to work anyway and stop
bothering you during your workout. Apparently I have a client
in a few minutes."

Lou wiped down the machine, then looked at Steve before
she went on to her next exercise. "What do you mean? What
client?"

"Oh, didn't I tell you? I'm the new trainer. Personal training
and boot camp. I was getting bored at home, and it just so
happened that they needed a trainer. I like Ann—she's nice."

"You *work* here?"

"Yeah. It's cool, right?"

"Yeah, sure."

"Are you sure? You don't look like it's okay." Steve touched Lou's arm but Lou took a step back. Steve looked at her curiously.

"Yeah, it's fine. I just have to...I have to go finish my workout. I gotta go." Lou retrieved her water bottle and left the gym, hoping Steve wouldn't follow. She went out to the main room and over to the wall where the Wing Chun wooden dummies were located, set her bottle on the floor, and began to practice her moves on a dummy, almost in a feverish fashion. As she was doing her movements, her pace picked up and she was able to block out the noises in the gym, as well as the ones in her head.

When Lou finished hitting the dummy, she decided to call it a day. She turned to go and saw Steve standing near the door, with her arms crossed over her chest, with a curious expression on her face. "Shit," she whispered. She walked to where Steve stood, in a mood for a confrontation.

When she reached her, Steve touched Lou's arm again to stop her. Lou's eyes traveled to Steve's hand, then back up to Steve's face and Steve let go. "Please tell me what's wrong. I know something is."

Lou exhaled, then shook her head. "I thought you understood about this place."

"What, that it's one of your favorite places? Yes, I get that."

"No, I don't think you do. I just need something that's mine."

"What, are you saying you don't want me working here?" Steve's voice started to lose its notes of sympathy and take on hints of incredulousness.

Lou put her hand on her forehead and shook her head. "It's hard to explain. I just...I need to go." Lou moved to leave, but Steve called her back.

"Lou, just say it. I invaded your space and you don't want me here. That's it, isn't it?"

Lou turned in Steve's direction, feeling sad and tired, and said, "I have no right to tell you where to be." Then she left the building and walked out to her Jeep, only realizing once she had slammed her door that she had left her street clothes in her locker, along with her keys and cell phone. She slammed her palm on the steering wheel and hollered out, "Fuck!" then leaned her head back on the seat, wondering how long she'd have to sit there before she could go back inside and retrieve them.

CHAPTER TEN

Lou arrived half an hour early to Bill and Dix's place on Thanksgiving Day, hoping to catch Bill alone for a moment, but no such luck. He was in the kitchen fussing over everything, insisting that he didn't need any help. For his contribution, Dix had made the pies and the rolls and set the table, then had gotten out of the kitchen as quickly as he could. He handed Lou a beer when she came in and ushered her to the living room with an expression that said, *Let's get out of his way.* Lou smiled in understanding and took the hint, leading the way into the living room, where they sat down on the couch.

"So, how many people are coming over this year?"

Dix took a sip of his wine and said, "Well, besides you, there's our friend Tony, who hasn't missed a Thanksgiving in six years. You met him last year."

"The guy with the beard, wearing the cardigan and the..." Lou made a gesture to indicate a large stomach.

"Yep, that's the old bear. Some years he brings a boyfriend, but he's flying solo this year. Then there's a new guy from my department. His name's Kevin, and he teaches Irish history."

"Oh, neat."

"Yes. He seems like a cool guy. Divorced. He doesn't talk about it much—I think he's still grieving. Then last but not least, you'll get to meet our daughter, Mona." Dix's face beamed at the mention of his daughter.

"Oh my God, that's awesome! I thought she lived in San Francisco?"

"She does, just like her namesake, but she missed the holidays last year because, as she put it, a PhD program is a lot of work and there's no such thing as a vacation. But she graduated in May and she's teaching now, so finally, she can take some time away."

"Her namesake?" Lou asked, confused.

"Mona Ramsey." Lou still didn't look any more enlightened. Dix rolled his eyes. "Oh my God, seriously? How can you be our friend and not know one of the most famous characters from classic gay literature?"

"Classic gay literature?"

"The *Tales from the City* series! There is more in the gay canon than *The Well of Loneliness* and *Rubyfruit Jungle*, you know? The boys have books too."

Lou smiled. "Yes, I'm aware of that, but do you think I have a lot of time to read? Besides my classes, there's the kung fu, my research, my writing, Steve…" Lou's voice trailed off and she looked away, then took a drink of her beer.

"Yes, how is that going? We have a few minutes before the others arrive and I have to play hostess. Talk to me."

Lou played with a loose thread in the seam of her cargo pants and sighed, not meeting Dix's eyes for a minute. Then, "It's okay. I don't know, it's getting weird." She shrugged and tried to give him a smile, but didn't quite make it.

"Weird how? Like, has she tried to tie you to the bed or something? Wants you to play…war games. Wink, wink, nudge, nudge." Dix lightly nudged her in the side with his elbow and gave her an elaborate wink.

That made Lou laugh, and she was grateful. "Why does weird have to mean something sexual? Besides, we haven't even gotten that far yet."

"Really? How many weeks has it been?"

"Three, I think?"

"You're asking me? Three weeks and you haven't sealed the deal yet? No wonder it's gotten weird. Bill and I barely waited three hours."

"Yes, well I'm not you, love."

"Obviously. So tell me how it got weird."

"It's nothing really. I mean, it'll sound stupid if I say it out loud."

"Try me."

"Well, she showed up at the Wushuguan yesterday. Apparently, she works there now. I had trouble processing her there, in my space. I kinda flipped out and left her standing there, wondering why I was mad. And, honestly, I couldn't really have said at the time, just that I didn't want her there because it's *my* space. I told you it was weird."

"Oh, honey, no, it's not. And I think I even understand it. It's your sanctuary. Not just a place where you go to be alone with your thoughts, but it makes you feel safe, doesn't it?" Dix looked at her tenderly.

It was all Lou could do not to start crying at his kindness. "Yeah, I think that's it. I've been taking kung fu since I was a teenager, you know? It was always a place I could go, a place where I felt strong and where I could take care of myself. Thank you, Doctor, I think you've cracked the case."

"Oh, come here, hon." Dix opened his arms and she went into them gratefully. She sniffed back tears as his arms tightened around her.

"What'd I miss?" Their embrace was broken up by Bill coming back into the room.

Lou sat back and wiped her eyes. "Nothing, I was just so happy he wasn't cooking today, it brought tears to my eyes." Lou gave Dix a smile and he laughed appreciatively.

"Uh-huh. You'll tell me about this later, young lady." Bill pointed an accusing finger at Lou and she nodded to him. Then he looked at Dix. "While you were in here feeling up our current lesbian, the other one called."

"Oh, how is our cast of *The Children's Hour* doing?"

Lou couldn't help but correct him. "I think you mean *Mädchen in Uniform*. *The Children's Hour* was about two teachers, not a teacher-student relationship."

Dix turned around with a smirk. "There are so many movies that end with a dead lesbian. How can I possibly keep up?"

"*Mädchen* doesn't end that way."

"Regardless, I'm sure it wasn't happy."

"Hello, Siskel and Ebert," Bill said, "are you two going to talk about the state of lesbian cinema all night, or do you want to hear about Maggie and Rory?"

"Oh, yes, sorry, love. How are they?"

Bill looked at Dix. "They're fine. Both families are up for the holiday, so she didn't have long to talk. Rory was doing all the cooking, as usual. The rest was just work stuff. Point being, they're good."

"Are they going to be in town for Christmas?"

"No, they're going to Boston. But they will head this way for New Year's."

"Wonderful, they're going to make the party then." Dix turned to Lou. "You'll get to finally meet your predecessor and her young hoyden. They're awesome—you'll love them."

"Between Rachel and you two, I've heard a lot about them. I'm sure you're right." Lou smiled at them, finally feeling a little better. Before any more could be said, the doorbell rang and Bill went to answer it. Lou put on a happy face and hoped her eyes didn't show that she had been crying.

Chapter Eleven

Friday morning, Lou decided to run by the Wushuguan before going to her office. She was going to take advantage of the quiet building, with everyone gone for the holiday, to get caught up on a few things. But first things first. She needed to talk to Steve. She arrived a few minutes before Steve's shift started, so Lou tried the locker room first, hoping to get Steve alone, but after checking the lockers, the showers, and the stalls, she discovered Steve was not to be found in there. She sighed, then went to the back of the building toward the gym. Steve was there, in the back corner, hitting the heavy bag. Before she approached her, Lou decided to watch her for a moment. Steve moved with the swift grace of a prize fighter; her punches came hard and fast, and each time Steve's fist made contact with the canvas, Lou winced. The power and ferocity with which Steve went at her task frightened Lou and it made her hesitate where she stood.

Finally, Steve stopped, bent down to the floor and picked up a water bottle, and drank from it. It was then when Lou took a step near her. "Hey." Lou's hands were behind her back and her head was slightly inclined.

Steve turned at the sound of her voice, bringing the bottle down to her chest. Cautiously, she said, "Hello."

Lou took another step forward. "You got a minute?"

"I have a couple."

"I'm sorry for acting weird the other day. I do owe you an explanation when you have time for one. I just want you to know, it isn't about you, you did nothing wrong, but I'm sorry if I made you think you did."

Steve took a step toward her. "Do you always apologize this much?" She seemed to be trying not to smile.

"Not usually."

"Don't make a habit of it. You apologized at the beginning—that was enough. I'd really like to hear that explanation. My shift ends at six."

"That sounds…oh, crap. We're expected at Bill and Dix's at eight."

"You still want me to go to that?"

Lou took one more step forward, closing the last bit of the gap between them. "I'd like you to, but I'll understand if you don't want to."

Steve grinned. "This is not the attitude of the badass I fell for."

"No?"

"No."

"So what would a badass do?"

"Now, I can't tell you that. If I did, then it wouldn't be very badass of you, would it?"

"True. Okay. My place, seven forty-five. Be sure to look cute. Oh, and a host gift would not be out of the question."

Grin still in place, Steve replied, "Yes, ma'am."

Lou gave her a small smile and turned to go, but Steve called her back.

"We'll talk after?"

"Of course." Lou left, passing her sifu on the way out, and exchanging a nod. She felt better about where she had left things with Steve, but dreaded the impending conversation.

❖

"You think they like me?" Steve asked, as she made the turn from Bill and Dix's street that would take her closer to campus.

Lou smiled. "You mean when Dix said, *When you two get married I want to officiate*, that wasn't a clue?"

"I thought he was just being silly."

"True, he's always being silly, but he was serious too. You want to hear what Bill said to me before we left?"

"I was wondering what you two were whispering about." Steve reached over and squeezed Lou's hand for a moment before she made a turn.

"He said, *You have my blessing*, like he was my father or something." Lou started to chuckle, but it fell flat and she let it taper off. "Where are we going?"

"I thought we could go to that little duck pond you showed me. Is that okay? Or would you prefer someplace more private?"

Lou gave her a smile and put her hand on Steve's knee. "No, its fine. It's a pretty place."

Steve found a parking space not too far from the pond and pulled in.

When they got out of the car, a light breeze blew past and Lou hugged her arms to herself and said, "I wish I'd remembered a jacket."

Steve reached in the back seat and rummaged around until she found a zippered fleece jacket, which she placed on Lou's shoulders. "Will this work?"

Lou gave her a grateful smile as she slipped her arms into the sleeves. "Perfect, thank you."

"The least I can do for dragging you outside on a chill November evening."

"No, as I said, this is perfect. Besides, I think this small pond has heard a lot of stories in its time. No reason why it shouldn't bear witness to mine." Lou inclined her head toward the water. "Come on." She held her hand out for Steve and Steve took it.

After they had walked for a bit, Steve looked up at the night sky. "The stars are out. And look how the moon bounces off the water. It's nice."

"Mm, it is. Did you know the early settlers used to call the November moon the Beaver Moon?"

Steve chuckled. "No, I did not. How and why do you know that?"

"It's not what you think."

"What am I thinking?"

"Mm-hmm." Steve laughed. "Anyway, they call it that because November is apparently the best time of the year to set beaver traps."

Steve gave a sly grin. "I'll try to remember that."

"Pervert." Steve chuckled. "As I was saying, I know that because one of my favorite books as a kid was the *Farmers' Almanac*."

"Were your family farmers?" Steve inquired.

"No, my father just always liked to read it. I don't know why. And I did what he did. He read it, so I read it."

"So you were close to your father?"

"For a while."

"What happened?"

Lou took a deep breath. "Until high school, he and I were inseparable. He could never get out of the house without me tagging along. He even started taking me to the shooting range. That's why I'm such a good shot. He taught me well. But by the time I was a sophomore, all that changed." Lou stopped talking and looked up at the moon again, somewhat wistful.

"What happened?" Steve asked, giving Lou's fingers a reassuring squeeze.

"The Gulf War."

"Oh, yes."

"It wasn't his first war, that was Vietnam. He was a career man. But there had been enough time since Vietnam, and enough therapy, that he was a good dad when I was growing up. We used to lie out in the backyard and he would teach me the stars."

Lou pointed up to a grouping of stars and said, "That's Pisces. I always like to look for that one, since it's my mother's sign." Lou took hold of Steve's arm and pointed at another clustering of stars. "And that's Cassiopeia over there. There are others, but those were always my favorites. According to myth, Cassiopeia was put in the sky by Poseidon as a punishment for boasting that she was more beautiful than the Nereids."

Steve smiled affectionately at Lou and leaned into her. "What were the Nereids?"

"Sea nymphs. Poseidon's wife was one. Needless to say, he didn't appreciate the boast."

"Doesn't sound like it."

Lou sighed. "I was always glad that I got to grow up with him when he was still like that. It could have been much worse."

"Yeah. The Gulf War changed him?"

"Yes. It reactivated his PTSD. When he came home, he didn't seek treatment and it took a while before we knew what was going on."

"What happened?"

Lou stopped walking and let go of Steve, and walked a little closer to the water, hugging her arms to herself again. Steve followed. "Did you know this pond has a name?"

"Lou." Steve put her hand on Lou's back.

"They call it Lake Van Horn, after the first college president. He was some kind of scientist before someone decided he should run the place. Geologist, I think. Or was it ecology? I can't remember."

"Lou, you were talking about—"

"They say he would often teach class out here. And, according to rumor, skinny-dip every full moon. Kids still do it sometimes, I've heard. Campus security doesn't mind, as long as they don't get too rowdy." Lou stopped talking abruptly, and there was a catch in her voice.

Steve put her arm around her shoulders. "Lou, what happened to your father after he came home from the Gulf?"

She turned to face Steve. "He was angry. That's how his PTSD manifested. He was angry at all of us. He…he started to get aggressive with me. Little things at first. Grabbing my arm roughly if he thought I mouthed off to him, smacking me on the back of the head if I didn't do something he told me to do right away. Then, a few months later, he hit me for the first time. Punched me square in the face. Broke my nose. I told everyone at school I fell while rock climbing. They had no reason not to believe me. A few weeks later, I came in ten minutes late for curfew. I had to stop for gas because I knew I couldn't bring the car back without a full tank. When I came in, he grabbed my arm and pulled real hard. I tried to yank it free and he just held on tighter and twisted, then slammed me into the wall. I heard it break. He did too, and that's when he stopped. He looked down at me like he was disgusted with me, then walked out of the room. Mom came in and didn't say anything, not about what happened. She just took me to the hospital."

"Oh, honey. I'm so sorry you had to go through that."

Lou chuckled softly. "But wait, there's more. While I was healing, my father didn't talk to me at all. I like to think he was ashamed of what he did and couldn't look at me. But he never apologized. I told my mom I wanted to learn self-defense and the local Wushuguan offered classes. She paid for them, then the kung fu classes I asked for later on. We never told my father. Several months later, he was drunk and I happened to walk through the living room at the wrong time, I guess, and he yelled at me to get out and told me to stop making so much noise. I hadn't been doing anything noisy. I apologized and started to walk out of the room, but he stood up and put his arm out to stop me and got in my face and started yelling. I'd had enough of his bullshit. I waited until he tried to hit me, then I grabbed his arm and held him there. I threatened to break *his* arm if he tried to hit me again. He called me a bitch and tried to get out of the hold. I warned him. I didn't want to do it, but I didn't want any more broken bones either. I put my other hand on his elbow and bent it sideways, kinda, until he was doubled over at the waist, and I pushed him all the way to the ground. It was sloppy because I hadn't been doing it that long, but it got the job done. I broke his wrist. I heard it snap and he hollered out. He called me something worse than a bitch. That stunned me more than anything. I let go and backed out of the room. He lay there crying. I heard him as I walked away." The wind came back and blew hair in Lou's face. Steve reached up and brushed it away. Lou leaned against Steve and Steve tightened her arm around her.

"I have no words."

"It's okay, I have plenty. He left us after that. Just up and left. We didn't know where he was and we didn't really look for him. Mom didn't divorce him, though, because she wanted me to go to college and the military would pay for it. A few years ago my mother received a letter from the Army about survivor's benefits."

"So your father's gone?"

"Yeah. He ended up with cirrhosis."

"Wow. What about your mom? Did she at least have a better life once he was gone?"

"Some. She didn't have to live with an abuser anymore. I knew I wasn't the only one he hit. I heard them. But I know she lived in fear even after he left, not knowing when or if he was coming back. So I don't think her life really started over until after she got that letter. But two years after she got it, she had a heart attack and died. So I guess you could say I'm an orphan." Lou tried to give Steve a wan smile but it didn't last.

Steve put both arms around Lou and kissed her on the forehead. "Baby, baby, baby…I wish I could have done something. But I'm so glad you were able to fight back. My little badass."

Lou chuckled and hugged her back and they stood that way for a long time, until Lou pushed Steve away gently and wiped her eyes. "The Wushuguan became my safe place. It was a place where he would never come, but even if he did, I knew I didn't have to deal with him."

Understanding dawned and Steve said, with recognition, "So when I showed up, I destroyed your sense of safety. Oh, God, I'm sorry."

"Baby, you didn't know. Don't apologize. It's just something I have to get over. I know he's gone and I'm safe. And if I run into anyone else who wants to treat me like that, I know I can handle it. I know it, in here." Lou pointed to her head. "But I'm still working on knowing it in here." She pointed to her heart.

"Of course. I understand."

"I really don't want to push you away."

"You haven't. And you won't. This solider holds her ground."

Lou, motioning to the small mound of grass beneath her feet, smiled and said, "But, Steve, I have the high ground."

Steve laughed. "Yeah, but that only matters in the movies." Steve caressed Lou's cheek, then very gently kissed her on the lips. "Come on, geek, let me take you home. It's getting chillier."

Lou chuckled. "Maybe you should have brought a jacket."

"What a great idea." Steve slipped her arm around Lou's waist as they walked back to the car.

❖

Steve took Lou home and walked her to her front door. On her doorstep they hugged for a long time, then Steve kissed her on the cheek and said. "You going to be okay tonight?"

"I think so. Thank you. But I'd be lying if I said I didn't need a drink right now. I won't, but I feel like I need one. I think I'll take a long bath instead and put some music on. I'll be okay." Lou managed a small smile for Steve's benefit.

"If you want to talk more, just call me. I'll stay up all night if you need me to."

"You're very sweet." Lou placed a soft kiss on Steve's lips, then lingered for a moment. When she stepped back, she asked, "Are you sure you don't want to come in?"

Steve sighed, then gave her a small smile. "I very much do

want to come in, but I won't. Now's not the time. But I promise, if you ask me that question on a happier day, I'll say yes."

"Steve Adams, you're old-fashioned," Lou said with delight.

"Maybe so. I don't know any other way to be."

"Well, I like it. Thank you." Lou kissed her again.

Steve groaned. "I need to go. But I meant what I said—call me if you need to."

"I will. Good night, Steve."

"Good night, Lou." Steve left the porch and walked to her car, then paused with her hand on the door handle and looked back. She smiled and waved, then got in her car. She waited until Lou unlocked her door and went inside before she pulled away.

Lou went inside, locking the door behind her, and went straight to her room. She kicked off her shoes next to the bed and took her glasses off and put them on the nightstand, then lay back on her pillows and put her hands on her stomach. Other than her mother, no one else knew about her father. She had never mentioned it to another girlfriend before—it had never really come up.

Telling Steve felt right. It brought them closer, and she wished she was with her now to curl up next to her, but Steve was probably right about that too. If she had her in bed next to her, it might lead to sex, and this just would not have been the right time for that. Books and movies often did that, put the vulnerable woman in a situation that ended in sex and made it seem like that was okay, but Lou always hated when they did that. It was an asshole move. She appreciated that Steve had enough sense to back away from that. She smiled now thinking of it.

She waited a few more minutes, when she figured Steve would be home and not driving, and sent a text. *Thank you for listening to me. It means a lot to me that you're not put off by any of this.*

I'm not going anywhere.

Good.

Don't forget, you have tougher trials than your childhood

ahead of you... We are having dinner with my mother on Sunday, remember?

Haha. Yes, I remember. I'm not worried. Your mother loves me.

Yes, she does.

Good night again. I think I'm going to go have that soak now.

You have a good night too.

Lou put the phone on her nightstand, smiling now, and sat up. She quickly undressed, throwing her clothes into the corner, then picked her phone back up as she walked to the bathroom. She selected some music, then set the phone on the counter. As she was adjusting the faucets on the tub, Beth Hart started to sing "Learning to Live." Another slow bluesy number was playing as she slid into the water. Lou settled in, letting the water and the music cover her like a soothing blanket, and closed her eyes and concentrated on the blues.

CHAPTER TWELVE

On Sunday, Lou drove to Steve's house, trying not to feel too nervous. It wasn't as if she was meeting Mrs. Adams for the first time. This wasn't even the first time today that they would be seeing each other, considering she had had a lesson with her that morning. But this was different and she knew it. She hadn't met her as Steve's mother before and she was worried about being assessed in this new way. Quite frankly, she worried about being good enough for Steve, even though she knew that was silly. She tried to get back the bravado and confidence she had displayed the night before in her text to Steve. After she pulled into Steve's driveway, she took a deep breath and said to herself, "You got this," then exited the Jeep.

Steve answered the door after she rang the bell and said a very simple "Hi" before she pulled her into a hug. Steve whispered in her ear, "You'll be fine," then gave her one last squeeze and a kiss on the cheek before standing aside and having her come in the house.

Lou noticed the boot tray by the door and just in general how neat everything was. She immediately felt the urge to go home and vacuum. But instead of fleeing the scene, she felt Steve's hand in hers as they went into the kitchen where Lorraine was busy finishing up their meal. She turned when they came into the room and gave Lou a smile. Lou returned it. "Hello, Mrs. Adams."

Lorraine used a cooking utensil for emphasis when she said, "Now, there won't be any of that here. It's bad enough I can't get you to call me by my name during my lessons, but here it sounds like an Eddie Haskell routine, and I don't won't any part of it, you hear me? In this house you will call me Lorraine or maybe eventually *Mom* if it suits you. But I'm not Mrs. Adams here. You understand me?"

Lou relaxed and said, "I do. I'll try my best."

"Good. Stephanie, are you going to just stand there, or are you going to offer her a drink? Don't act like I didn't teach you manners."

"Yes, ma'am." Steve winked at Lou, who was biting her lip to keep from giggling. "Would you like a drink?"

"Sure. Water's fine."

Lorraine turned back around. "No, it's not. If you'd rather have a beer, go ahead and say so. I'm going to have one. Though I promised Stephanie I wouldn't get sloshed and embarrass her." Lorraine winked at her daughter.

"Mother, you made me no such promise," Steve said, as she pulled a beer out of the fridge and held it aloft for Lou, asking with a look if she'd prefer that instead. Lou nodded, and Steve handed it to her.

"I didn't? Oh, good."

"You did, however, promise not to embarrass me. I think that would qualify."

"I don't recall any such promise. I think you have me confused with someone else. Now set the table."

Steve went to the cabinet to retrieve the plates and Lou went to her to offer her help, but Lorraine caught her. "Oh, no, you are a guest today—let us serve you. You'll be a member of this family soon enough. Take advantage of the star treatment while you have it."

Lou chuckled. "All right." She took a seat and watched as Steve brought plates and silverware to the table. She caught her eye and smiled, and Steve put her hand on Lou's shoulder and squeezed on her way by.

Lorraine set the pan of lasagna and a bowl of salad in the middle. "I hope you like Italian."

"Mom never forgave Grandmother for being British and not Italian. Pasta is all she makes."

"And I'm damn good at it too."

"Yeah, but the carbs, Mom. A lot of extra gym time with every meal."

"I see you've somehow managed." Lorraine turned to Lou conspiratorially. "She looks good, doesn't she?"

Lou tried not to choke on her words. Good thing she hadn't taken a bite yet. She saw Steve's cheeks redden. "She does."

"I don't know where she gets her drive from. Neither her father nor I was athletic to save our lives. We were porch sitting people from way back. They used to call it mellow back in the day. We were readers too. I still am, of course."

"Me too, Lorraine, though I haven't had much time to read lately."

Lorraine smiled knowingly toward her daughter. "I'll bet."

"Mother!"

"We're all adults here. And I wasn't implying anything other than I know you two have been spending a lot of time together."

Steve grinned sheepishly. "Like hell you weren't."

Lorraine turned to Lou again. "She has been treating you right, I assume? Don't be afraid to tell me if she hasn't."

Lou smiled across at Steve, then looked at Lorraine. "She has had perfect manners. Always courteous and respectful. And sometimes quite charming."

Lorraine was obviously proud of her daughter. "Well, good, I'm glad the old lessons haven't faded. That's something she gets from her father, though. He was such a gentleman. Oh, that man. Always doing all the old-fashioned things, like holding doors and pulling out my chair. Letting me go ahead. And standing back grinning like a cat whenever I shot my mouth off about something. He used to say, *Girl, I like your spunk*, like he was Lou Grant, you remember? Oh, look at me, you've barely just arrived and I'm already getting sentimental." She wiped the corners of her eyes, and Steve reached over and took her mother's hand for a moment and they shared a smile.

"I think Mr. Adams would be very proud of his daughter."

"Oh, and he was. He never understood why she joined the military, though. We were and have always been pacifists, but we wanted her to make her own decisions. He used to show anyone who asked after her her graduation photo. You know, the one with the full dress green uniform? I was so glad when she switched to dress blues. Olive drab was never a good color for anyone. Did you see the picture on the wall when you came in?" Lorraine asked Lou.

Smiling, Lou said, "No, I missed it."

"Here, let me get it." Lorraine pushed her chair out.

"Mother, sit down. You can show her later."

"I might forget later. Eat your food, I'll be right back." She walked out to retrieve her quarry.

Steve looked over at Lou and shook her head with a smile. Lou suppressed her giggles.

Lorraine came back a moment later holding an eight-by-ten wooden frame and handed it to Lou. Lou wiped her mouth and put her fork down, then took the frame from her. She smiled at the image of a much younger Steve with collar-length blond hair, shining blue eyes, and a radiant smile, her new green dress uniform looking stiff and proper. She looked across at Steve and saw that she was trying not to blush or look anxious about her reaction. Finally, she said, "You were adorable."

"Still is, isn't she?"

"Very true."

"That picture doesn't show how scared I was. I shipped out to Bosnia shortly after graduation," Steve said quietly.

"You haven't told me about that yet."

"I will, someday. I also went to Iraq part deux." Steve gave her a small smile, then shifted her gaze. "Mom, put that away, would you? We're still eating."

"Yes, of course." She took the picture from Lou and took it back to the living room. When she returned, she had a smile on her face. "So, Lou, I can't say that I understand exactly what it is that you teach."

"Oh, I thought I had told you. I teach stage combat mostly, but also stage direction and dramaturgy. In the spring, I get stuck with an undergrad intro class. My boss joked that it was paying my dues. Really, he just couldn't rope anyone else into it." Lou smiled.

"What was that word you said? It sounded like *drama turd*."

"Gross, Mom!"

Lou almost choked on her food. She grabbed her napkin and held it to her mouth while she swallowed. She coughed slightly, then took a drink.

"What? It's a perfectly legitimate question. Are you okay, dear?"

"I'm fine. Yes, it is a legit question. The word was drama*turgy*, with a *g*."

"And what is that, exactly?"

"A dramaturge can serve many functions in a theater, from research, to editing, to helping cast, as well as many other things the director might need them to do. They basically have to know about every aspect of the behind-the-scenes stuff because they could be called upon to help with any or all of it. It's a fun thing to do, but a lot of responsibility."

"Have you done it yourself?" Steve asked.

"A few times. I've always enjoyed it."

"So, it's kinda like a girl Friday?"

"Well, sort of, I guess." Lou smiled at Lorraine.

"Sounds like a lot of fuss and bother to me, especially when you have to be at the beck and call of some temperamental director. Not for me, thanks. I'll keep pushing books."

"Mother, you make being a librarian sound like a drug dealer."

"I'm just offering a different kind of high." Lorraine leaned over to Lou in a conspiratorial manner and stage-whispered, "Hey, kid, wanna get something that'll really make your mind drift away? Something that'll make you forget about the world around you?" Lou giggled and Steve rolled her eyes.

"Well, when you put it that way, I guess I'm an addict then." Lou laughed but noticed Steve suddenly got interested in her food and Lorraine's smile faltered.

"Yes, well, I shouldn't have made that kind of joke." She glanced at Steve. "I'm sorry."

Steve gave her a brief smile. "It's okay. Book pusher."

Lorraine visibly relaxed. "Well, who's ready for dessert? I made lava cakes. Not very Italian, admittedly, but who doesn't like molten hot chocolate?"

"That sounds wonderful."

"Good. Stephanie, clear the table while I serve, would you?" Lorraine favored her daughter with a smile before she left the table.

"Sure." Steve stood to do as her mother asked. When she reached for Lou's plate, Lou took her free hand and squeezed, rubbing her thumb over the top. Steve reached down and kissed her on the forehead, then picked up her plate and took it to the sink.

Lou stayed maybe another hour after dessert was over, but then she had to get going, as it was a school night. "Thank you, Lorraine. I'm glad I got to know you in this way and I hope to have more dinners like this."

"Oh, you can count on it. I have tons more pictures to show you, and a lifetime of embarrassing stories to tell. I don't care what she says—it's my right and duty."

"Yes, it is. And you will always find me a willing audience." She extended her hand. "See you next Saturday, as usual."

"Put that away. You're family now. Come here." Lorraine

opened her arms for a hug and Lou laughed and accepted the gesture.

"Okay, I really must go. Thanks again. Steve?"

"Yeah, I'll walk you out. Mother will stay here and pretend not to watch out the window." Steve put her hand on the small of Lou's back as she ushered her to the door.

"No use pretending now, is there?" Lorraine smiled affectionately at Steve.

Steve just shook her head as she led Lou out to her car. Once outside and out of earshot, Lou leaned against her Jeep and Steve leaned in close to her and took both her hands in hers. "Sorry if that got intense sometimes. You held your own, though. My mother can be a lot to handle sometimes."

"Maybe for you. I told you she loves me." Lou gave her a cocky smile and it made Steve laugh. "I had a good time. I loved seeing your graduation photo. You were more than adorable, though."

"Oh?"

Lou removed her hands from Steve's and put them around her neck and Steve put her arms around Lou's waist. "Yeah. Very sexy. Just something about a girl in uniform…"

Steve raised an eyebrow, then leaned in for a kiss.

"Steve?"

"Yes?"

"Anytime you want to talk about your service, I'll listen. I hope you know that."

"Yeah, I do. I'll tell you all my secrets, in time. I'm in no rush."

"Me neither. Okay, soldier, you better go help your CO do the dishes before you get court-martialed."

"How bad can it be? I already have KP duty. I'll text you later." Steve gave her one more kiss, a quick one this time, then reluctantly released her.

Lou squeezed her hand before letting go entirely, then got into her vehicle. She waved as she drove away.

When Steve went back inside, she found her mother in the kitchen, working on the dishes. "You started without me." She grabbed a dish towel out of a drawer and began her part of the job.

"Well, I wasn't going to wait forever," her mom said jovially.

"No, no, of course not."

They washed and dried in silence for a minute, then her mother said matter-of-factly, "You haven't told her about Cairyn yet."

"Not yet."

"Didn't think so. You plan to?"

"Yeah, I just gotta figure out how."

"I think she'll understand. I like her, Stephanie. I'm glad you're dating her."

Steve smiled. "Yeah. I like her too."

"I should hope so, after kissing her like that in the driveway."

"I knew you were watching." Steve pointed an accusatory finger at her.

"Of course I was. Had to make sure you didn't make a damn fool of yourself."

Steve threw back her head and laughed.

Steve's cell rang at four something in the morning. Groggily, she answered, without checking the caller ID. "Hello?"

"Sgt. Adams?"

Steve recognized the gruff voice instantly and sat up, her mind quickly clearing. "First Sgt. Richards."

"Sorry to wake you, but I just took an emergency call from the Red Cross."

Panicking, Steve threw off her covers and put her feet on the floor. "Is it my mother? Is she okay?" Ever since the death of her father the year before, she'd been worried about how her mother was getting on. She wished she could be there to help her through her grief, but duty called. Duty always called.

"Your mother is the one who contacted the Red Cross, actually. This was concerning someone named Cairyn."

"Cairyn? What's wrong? What happened to Cairyn?" Picturing car crashes and other accidental calamities, Steve wasn't prepared for what came next, though she should have been.

The man whose job it was to be a hard-ass suddenly sounded reluctant to deliver the rest of the news he had called for. "Well, it seems…according to your mother, Ms. Williams passed away earlier today. Funeral services are being arranged. As soon as that's settled, we'll get you home."

Steve barely heard him. She mumbled her thanks and accidently called him *sir*. He didn't comment on it. She hung up and numbly put the phone back on her nightstand. She knew what had happened without him having to say it. Cairyn had succeeded this time. Her first sergeant didn't have any other details and Steve knew it was because her mother had been discreet. Bless her. What she wanted to do was scream, but she didn't want to wake anyone. Instead, she grabbed her pillow and held it up to her face and screamed into it, though it didn't muffle things completely. Her roommate stirred in her bunk and turned to look at her.

"You okay?" she asked, half asleep.

Steve couldn't answer her. She started dry heaving and then rocking back and forth. Her roommate got out of her bunk and sat down beside her and put her arm around her shoulders. That was all it took to break the dam. The tears started to flow. Gut-wrenching sobs tore at her as she cried into the pillow. Eventually, she collapsed against her roommate, a woman by the name of Regina, who had pictures of her children taped to the wall above where she laid her head at night. She would kiss them good night every night and go to sleep with a smile. It was to her maternal nature Steve turned now. Regina held her until morning, not knowing what had happened until the tears finally stopped sometime around sunrise, when Steve could finally articulate her thoughts. *The first thing she said was, "Cairyn's gone. Oh God, Cairyn's gone."*

"Cairyn's gone, Cairyn's gone." Steve twisted and turned in her covers, waking herself up with the sound of her own voice. She sat up, breathing heavily, and threw the covers off. Her heart was beating rapidly and she was starting to feel out of control. She groped on the nightstand in the dark, not bothering to turn on the lamp, until her fingers felt the cool metal of the chain, and she picked it up and brought the Capricorn pendant to her mouth and kissed it, then took a deep breath. She started to calm and she felt her heartbeat start to normalize again. Then she put the chain back around her neck and lay back down, staring off into space as she fingered the symbol of Cairyn's birth, trying not to think of her death.

Instead, she remembered the night they'd met. She had been stationed in Ft. Sill, Oklahoma, at the time, training the new female recruits. She had the weekend off and had been invited to a party off base by one of the other female sergeants, another lesbian. The party was at the woman's house and she had invited all the lesbians she knew on base, as well as some local women. Steve hadn't been there long, only long enough to know that there wasn't much of a gay scene there, so she welcomed the chance to hang out with other lesbians and, possibly, the chance to get laid. It'd been a while. She dressed in nice slacks and a dark blue pinstripe men's shirt, cuffing the sleeves over a white T-shirt. She kept her dog tags on, between the shirts, thinking they might be a conversation starter later. She smiled to herself as she splashed on her cologne, hoping it would last for the duration, then checked her hair in the mirror one last time, making sure everything was in place, then headed out the door.

After making small talk with the hostess, she walked around the house with a bottle of beer in hand, holding it lazily by the neck, scanning the crowd. Within the first hour, all the single people seemed to be huddled up with partners, so Steve found a spot in the living room to lean against the wall, feeling a little sorry for herself. She wasn't there long before some woman came up to talk to her.

"You strike out too?" she asked, giving Steve an appraising smile.

"Not really." Steve gave the woman an appraising look of her own. She was taller than her, with awesome legs, which she was showing off in a light summer dress. Her hair went midway down her back, dark brown with corkscrew curls. Her brown eyes danced as she smiled at Steve and she wore a challenging expression, as if she was daring Steve to take action, make the first move, maybe.

She laughed. "I know, everyone's already coupled up. Some of these women work fast."

Steve laughed with her. "Yeah. I guess I like to take my time."

The woman gave Steve a sly look and asked, "Is that right, soldier?"

Steve inclined her head and grinned back. "It is. Especially on the things that matter."

The woman gave Steve a long look, then finally said, "I'll keep that in mind."

"Good. What's your name?"

"Cairyn. Yours?"

"Steve."

"Nice to meet you, Steve."

The music suddenly changed from the soft rock that had been playing to a Melissa Etheridge song. Steve smiled. "I know it's a cliché, but I do love me some Melissa."

"God, I know, she's hot."

"Would you like to dance?"

Eyes twinkling, Cairyn replied, "Yes, I would."

Steve set her beer down on a nearby table and held out her arms. Cairyn stepped into her embrace and they swayed in their small spot on the edge of the room, oblivious to everyone else. It was only fitting that they share their first kiss to "An Unusual Kiss." But there was nothing unusual about it. It was sweet and tender, and every year thereafter, on their anniversary, they made sure to dance to that song, kissing at the end of it.

Steve went back to sleep with a smile on her face, mumbling lines from the song, her fingers around the pendant.

❖

Lou knew she was dreaming. It started sweet. It was 1992, she knew that, because Ani DiFranco's *Imperfectly* album provided the soundtrack to her memories.

While the music played, loudly, she and her best friend, Tanya, were giggling about the song that was playing, "In or Out." They weren't laughing at the song, just what it very clearly implied. They had played the song over and over again, singing parts of it to each other, relishing in particular the line about having spots *and* stripes. That's how they saw themselves or, rather, how Tanya saw herself. Lou couldn't admit to her that she was all stripes. If she did, she feared she would lose the occasional make-out sessions she and Tanya sometimes engaged in in her room, always with music blaring. She might also lose her best friend, to say nothing of her secret becoming known. She couldn't risk it, so she kept it to herself and told herself to be grateful for the kisses she was sometimes able to steal. Just last week Tanya had let her touch her breast—briefly, outside her shirt, but it was something.

Tanya went up to the CD player on Lou's shelf and skipped the next two songs, until "If It Isn't Her" began to play. She cocked her head and looked at Lou and smiled and held her arms out. In a teasing way, she asked, "May I have this dance?"

Giggling, Lou accepted and stepped into her best friend's embrace. They swayed to the music naturally, as it wasn't the first time they had danced together. Lou felt like she was at a school dance as she swayed in her *Star Wars* socks, a gift from Tanya for her last birthday, barely moving, her arms around the girl whom she knew beyond a doubt she loved. She nuzzled Tanya and Tanya giggled.

"That tickles," she whispered.

"You like it," Lou teased.

"Mm-hmm, that does feel nice."

"I knew it," Lou whispered.

When Lou realized Tanya had put the song on repeat, she giggled and they continued to sway and kiss along to the music. Occasionally, Lou would sing softly to her, feeling with all her heart the message of the song applied to them. She was looking into Tanya's eyes when her bedroom door opened, and she saw her father standing in the doorway, a question dead on his lips and anger building in his eyes. Tanya backed away from Lou instantly, as if she'd been jolted by electricity.

Her father said in a controlled tone of voice, never taking his eyes off her, "Tanya, I think it's time you went home."

Tanya looked from him back to Lou. Lou gave her a small nod of encouragement and Tanya quickly left without a word. Before Lou could say anything, her father was upon her. He grabbed her upper arm roughly and spat out, "What the hell were you doing?"

"Dad, that hurts."

Her father gripped her tighter and she yelped in pain. "I don't give a damn if it hurts, you baby. What were you doing in here with her? Don't try to deny it, girlie!"

Lou's voice came out in a strangled cry and she hated herself for it. "Nothing!"

"I said, don't lie to me. You were doing queer things, weren't you? Weren't you?"

"No, Father." When the blow came, it was the last thing

she expected. His fist came swift and hard against her face and he released her, and she fell into a heap on her bedroom floor, clutching her bleeding nose and crying in pain.

"No child of mine is going to be queer. Girl or boy. You hear me? Now, I don't want to see that shit again. Go clean yourself up." With that, his final word on the subject, her father turned and left.

Lou groped around on the floor until she found a discarded T-shirt and held it to her bloody face. She wiped the tears from her cheeks with the back of her hand. She mumbled under her breath, "Fucking bastard," vowing to herself that she wouldn't let anything like that happen again.

The next day at school, everyone believed her story about rock climbing. Everyone except Tanya. She looked at her sympathetically and even came up to her and caressed her cheek, but pulled back quickly to make sure no one saw them. That was the last time she and Tanya were ever alone in her room together. And it was the last time they ever shared a kiss. Tanya started to distance herself from Lou after that, but Lou, though heartbroken, wasn't mad about it. Tanya was doing what she was doing for Lou's own good. Lou figured it was for the best, as she knew that until she was older and on her own, she couldn't show affection at home, not with her dad around.

CHAPTER THIRTEEN

Lou woke up the next morning feeling out of sorts, though she wasn't sure why. She had a vague idea of what she had dreamed about the night before, and if part of what she recollected was true, then she knew what the rest of her dream must have been. She rubbed her eyes and reached for her phone on the nightstand, checking the time: 7:50. Ten minutes before her alarm was set to go off. She canceled the alarm and set the phone back on her nightstand, then grabbed her covers and brought them back up to her chin, rolling over on her side. She was awake enough that she knew she wouldn't fall back asleep, but she didn't feel like moving yet. The prospect of actually putting her feet on the floor and starting her day seemed like a daunting task, one that was beyond her capabilities this Monday morning.

But it was the first day back after the holiday weekend and finals were only two weeks away. She had the panicked students who would be demanding her attention, as well as mounds of grading to look forward to.

"Ugh." She gave a disgusted, weary sigh as she flung the covers off and sat up, then reached for her glasses. No matter what type of frames she had, they always felt crooked on her nose, and her current thin wire ones were no exception. Sighing again, she stretched her arms out wide and leaned back, reveling in the movement of her muscles and the feel of her back popping. Finally, she smiled. "Good stretch."

She realized, as she walked to her closet to look for clothes, that what she needed to cheer herself up was a good dose of Bill. She knew where to find him this early, and she quickly got dressed and combed her unruly hair, putting it in a clip to keep it in place, then grabbed her bag off the kitchen chair and her keys off the table and left the house. She made a quick stop at her favorite coffee shop to grab herself a cup of Colombian and a sweet caramel concoction they made in-house, giving it some chichi froufrou name that Lou was almost embarrassed to even say, reminding her of those old IHOP commercials.

As she was waiting in line behind all the other people in a hurry to get to work, she heard the person behind her give a slight cough, almost as if they were trying to get her attention, even though it seemed unlikely that anyone else she knew would be there, especially that early. Next, she heard a voice behind her say, "This is your favorite place, isn't it, Dr. Silver?"

Surprised to hear her name from an unfamiliar voice, she turned around and came face to chin with a young woman with a short cropped blond haircut, definitely young enough to be one of her students. She didn't recognize her, though, and thought she must be a nonmajor who had taken her intro class last spring, or just another theater student who recognized her from the building. She was used to students, whether they had once been hers or had just seen her in passing, remembering her more often than she remembered them. After all, they outnumbered her. She smiled at the girl, trying to be polite. "I guess you could say that. I do come here quite a bit when I need a place to escape to."

"I know, I've seen you." The girl's smile remained in place.

It was almost flirtatious, Lou thought. She chalked it up to aging vanity and decided the girl was just being polite to a professor who was probably at least twenty years older than her. Lou nodded. "I'm not surprised."

"You don't remember me, do you?"

Lou looked chagrined. "Was I that obvious?"

The girl chuckled. "A little. I saw you in here a couple of months ago. You were sitting at that table in the back corner." She pointed to the table in question. "I was in uniform, not my civvies." She gestured to the jeans and T-shirt she was currently wearing with a grin. "It's no wonder you don't recognize me."

Lou smacked her forehead as the memory flashed. "Bolen! I do remember you."

"Yeah, that's right." Now there was no mistaking the drop in tone in the girl's voice—she was clearly going for flirtatious. "My first name's Mel. Kinda cool that you remembered me."

Lou recognized what was about to happen and smiled wanly but said nothing, not wanting to jump the gun in case the girl chickened out. She didn't want to give the speech if she didn't have to.

"I guess I should ask this before it's your turn and you're gone. Would you like to go out sometime?"

Lou looked at the girl with kindness when she said, "I'm sorry, I can't. I'm seeing someone. And, to be honest, I don't date students, either mine or someone else's." *Plus, I have T-shirts older than you.*

Mel visibly deflated for a moment, but she let it pass and smiled. "Ah, okay. Totally understand. I had to try."

Lou kept the smile plastered to her face. Thankfully, she was up next and she went to the counter and put her order in, then made a hasty retreat when it was completed, securing the drinks in the cup holders in her Jeep before heading to campus.

She parked in the lot next to the theater building, then grabbed her bag and her keys, along with the coffee, and headed down to the basement where Bill spent most of his time. The entire south wing of the basement was his lair. She knew where his workshop was, as most of the rest of the space was used for costume and prop storage. She headed to the room he referred to as his studio and found him bent over a large work table, working on a drawing of some kind, blaring Patsy Cline's "Crazy" at top volume. She walked up behind him, knowing he couldn't see or hear her, and started to sing along with the country icon. Bill turned around with a smile on his face.

"Well, hello there, sunshine. I do love your voice."

"Thank you. Here." She held out the cup of caramel concoction and he took it with a smile.

"For me? Oh, thank God, you must have seen the Bat-Signal I put up." He took the lid off and took a generous sip. "Oh, that is good."

"I knew you'd like it. I think it's equal parts sugar and coffee." Lou grinned, as she took a seat on a nearby stool, drinking her coffee.

"You know me well. You know I can't resist sweet things." He cuffed her gently on the chin with a wink.

"Aw, you're a sweetie. And a bullshitter."

"You say that like they're different." Bill placed the cup on the table where it wouldn't be in his way, then bent back over his drawing. "So, what brings you down to the dungeon?"

"I just wanted to see you. Feels like forever."

"Yes, a whole three days. I'm surprised you've lasted this long."

Lou laughed. "It's been difficult."

"Sgt. Hottie been taking up all your time?"

Amused, Lou asked, "Why do you keep calling her that?"

"Because it's true."

"I thought you weren't into girls?"

"Well, I never get *into* them"—Lou laughed—"but I can recognize beauty when I see it. It *is* my job, you know?" He held up the paper he was drawing on and showed it to Lou. "What do you think?"

It was an elegant flapper dress, Lou supposed it was called, black, and off one shoulder. "It's very lovely. Planning on wearing that to the New Year's Eve party, are you?"

Bill grinned and tapped her on the nose with his pencil. "Don't be ridiculous. You know our party's always informal."

"Ah, yes, of course. Pity, it would show off your legs."

"I know, wouldn't it? Maybe another time. So, my wayward little lesbian, why are you in my lair?"

"And why exactly am I wayward?"

"How would I know? I'm sure you've done something naughty recently. And if you have, I don't want to know about it. I don't know if my delicate sensibilities could handle it."

Lou snorted. "Delicate sensibilities? Excuse me, I must have wandered into the wrong lair. I was looking for Bill. Maybe you've seen him?"

"Maybe you took a wrong turn at Albuquerque."

She mocked laughing at him by opening her mouth wide and pointing at him, as if he had made a good joke. "No, I don't think so. Any turn I made leaving Albuquerque was the right turn."

"I forgot you grew up there. Your father was Air Force, right?"

"No, Army."

"Ah, just like soldier girl. I didn't know Albuquerque was known for Army."

"The reserves are there. He left active duty when I was a kid but stayed in the reserves. That's how much he loved it." Lou became lost in her own thoughts for a moment.

"You okay?" Bill, still bent over his drawing, making final adjustments, interrupted her musings.

"Yeah, I'm fine." She plastered a smile on her face and pointed to the drawing. "So if that's not for New Year's, what's it for?"

"Oh, yes, I didn't mention that part. We're doing *Chicago* next semester and this will be one of the costumes. Once we find an actress to wear it, of course." Suddenly, he picked the drawing up off the table and looked between Lou and the paper in his hand and grinned.

"Oh, no, I'm not wearing that thing."

"Oh, come on! You're an actress, you've got great pipes, and I think you would look hot in this. I'm sure your soldier girl will think so too."

"Well, thank you, I think, but those plays are a chance for the students to shine. Besides, I'm not exactly a Roxie Hart."

"No, you're not. And this isn't for Roxie—it's for Velma. You would make a great Velma. You can do sexy." Bill grinned like a cat as he appraised her.

"Gee, thanks. But if you think you're going to get me to wear that getup that has no crotch, you have got another thing coming." She was referring to the outfit worn in one of the musical numbers, the "Cell Block Tango."

"It has a crotch!" Then he mumbled, "Just a small one."

"Crotch floss is more like it. Careful, or you'll be the next one who has it coming." She grinned.

"Well, you're no fun. Think about it. Besides, how long has it been since you've been on stage?"

"Two years ago, at my last job. We staged *The Three Musketeers*."

"And which soldier were you, pray tell?"

"Isn't it obvious?"

"You don't mean…"

She shook her head and they said together, "D'Artagnan!"

"I bet you were the cutest thing."

"I did get to use a sword. Swords are fun."

"So for you, joining the military means wearing tights and prancing around on stage dressed like a playing card."

Lou laughed. "Yes, I guess you could say that."

"So have you worked out your issues with dating a vet? All jokes aside." Bill gave her a look of concern.

She sighed. "I'm getting there. It doesn't hurt that she's very sweet and seems to understand what I'm dealing with. I think she has something in her past too that she struggles with, but she hasn't talked about it yet. I wish she would, but all things in time, I guess."

"Right. Sweetie, I really do think she's the one. I think you got it right this time. I'm glad you're taking it slow. I know I joke about your sex life, but really, I'm glad you're letting this evolve into something stronger. You need this in your life." He smiled affectionately at her.

She stood and gave him a brief hug. After they separated, she said, "Thank you, and I agree with most of what you said. But I don't want to be with her because I need her—I want to be with her because I love her. I want to stand on my own in a relationship."

"True, but it's always nice to have someone to lean on once in a while when you get weary."

"Yeah." She sighed wistfully, then stood and grabbed her half-drunk coffee. "Well, I should get upstairs. Lots to do before I have to be in class today."

"Hiding in your office, don't you mean?"

"It's a living. I'll see you later." She waved casually to him and started to walk away.

"Oh, and don't think I didn't hear what you just said a moment ago. The question is, did you?" His question was said just as casually as her parting words.

She turned around, confused. "What are you talking about?"

He said nothing, just raised an eyebrow.

"I don't know what you're getting at, but I gotta go."

"Hmm. Let me know when you figure it out." He bent back to his work, erasing something on the paper, then redrawing it.

She just shook her head and left. She was halfway down the hallway before it came back to her and she remembered what it was she had said and what he had been alluding to. She knew her words made it sound as if she was in love with Steve, but that was not something she wanted to think about right now. Instead of pondering the implication of her words and analyzing it to death, she just shook her head and continued walking in the direction of the stairs, bypassing the ancient elevator that was so old it still had lead paint on the walls and often stalled between floors. Regarding the state of her relationship, she said to herself, "I don't have time for this," as she came upon the alcove where the stairs were and began her climb up to her office on the third floor.

❖

Back in her office, Lou was working on thinning out her email. When her phone buzzed she picked it up to read, *Hey, was just wondering if you have plans for lunch.*

She smiled and responded, *No, but I have a feeling I'm about to. What'd you have in mind?*

Meet me at the spot where you showed me Cassiopeia, at noon.

Lou chuckled in disbelief, shaking her head. "That woman…" *You have a date. Anything you want me to bring?*

You're enough.

Lou sighed contentedly. She sent back a smile, then replaced her phone on her desk, making sure to check the time before doing so. An hour to go. "Great, now how am I supposed to concentrate on this crap?" She shook her head once to clear out the thoughts that were starting to form and opened another email, trying to get back on task.

An hour later, she locked up her office and headed out to the lake to the spot where, just a few nights before, she had told Steve some of her long-held secrets, and pointed out the spot in the heavens where a vain sea nymph resided. She hurried over, quickening her pace for the short trek across the parking lot in front of the theater building, over the small hill, and it was there, next to a tree, that Steve stood, with a blanket spread out on the grass and a picnic basket sitting on top.

Steve was waiting for Lou with her back turned, looking out at the water.

Lou went up behind her and said, "Steve…this is wonderful."

Steve turned around at the sound of her voice and touched Lou's face, then placed a small kiss on her lips. Lou was careful not to get carried away, as it was the middle of the day and students were always near. "I'm glad you like it. I wasn't sure if you would want to get sloshed in the middle of the day, so instead of wine, I got sparkling grape juice. Is that okay?"

Lou laughed and gave her a peck on the lips. "Yes, that's fine. Come on, show me what's in your picnic basket. Just no feeding any cartoon bears, I don't care how cute they are." Lou pointed her finger at Steve in playful admonishment.

Steve laughed. "I'll try to resist, Boo Boo."

Lou stopped in her tracks and narrowed her eyes at Steve. "Really?"

"What? It's better than what the kids are calling their significant others."

"Is it really?"

"Sure, that bear was cute. And if truth be known, I think he was smarter than Yogi."

"Someone had to keep Yogi out of trouble. Is that my role in this relationship?"

"Somebody's gotta do it."

Lou sighed histrionically. "Fine, you can call me that, just not in front of my students. Or Bill. I think he'd be worse."

Steve nodded. "Deal. Boo Boo, it suits you. Now we'd better sit down before I make a scene."

"Good idea."

They took positions on the blanket, and Steve unpacked the food she had brought—a series of cheeses and cold cuts, as well as fresh fruit and the aforementioned sparkling grape juice.

Lou smiled over at Steve and said, "This was a great idea, I'm glad you thought of this."

"I am too. I like seeing you in the middle of the day. You look disheveled and real and maybe that doesn't sound like the most romantic thing I could say, but you look the way I imagine you look on any given day, instead of when you are all gussied up for a date, and I like it and I want to see you like this all the time. Just you being comfortable with yourself, doing all the things, and apparently teaching class in nylon cargo pants that show off the fact you have a nice ass."

Lou feigned shock. "So much for romantic. But my ass thanks you." She leaned forward and kissed her, then said, "That actually was very sweet."

"So when do you have to be back? How long do I get to keep you?"

"I don't have to be in class until two. Two hours long enough, soldier?" Lou gave Steve a look she hoped was flirtatious.

Steve's mischievous grin suggested success. "Depends on what we end up doing."

Lou raised an eyebrow. "Only time will tell." She leaned toward her and whispered, "But maybe it should tell soon. What do you think?"

Steve swallowed and whispered back, "I think you're right."

She ran her fingers down Lou's neck and Lou shivered under her touch. Lou brought her face closer for a long, slow, soft kiss. When they separated, Steve looked troubled.

"Something wrong?"

Steve brushed an errant curl off Lou's forehead and sighed. "I think, before we go any further, there's something you should know."

Lou pulled back some, as the romantic moment had passed, and put her hand on Steve's leg. "Okay, I'm listening."

Steve clasped Lou's fingers with hers and looked at their hands briefly, then back at Lou. "I think it's time I told you about Cairyn."

"All right," Lou said cautiously.

"Cairyn was my girlfriend. Well, after a few years, she became my fiancée. Not long after I deployed I got a call from my mother saying that Cairyn was in the hospital. She had OD'd on some leftover painkillers from when I hurt my back during a training exercise. It was nearly a full bottle—I didn't like being all drugged up and I decided to use exercise instead of pills to make it better. Anyway, she had taken nearly the whole bottle. She's lucky my mother had come by. They were supposed to go shopping that day. She was in the hospital for two weeks, had to have her stomach pumped and spend time on the psych ward and everything. When I was finally able to talk to her, you know what she said?"

Lou shook her head.

"She said, *I missed you. I couldn't stand the thought you might die. I didn't want to live without you.* I mean, I knew she didn't like the fact I was a soldier, I knew it scared her, but I never thought…" Lou tightened her fingers around Steve's and Steve gave her a grateful smile. "I couldn't exactly leave and come home. My mother stepped in. God, she was wonderful. She made it her mission to try to keep Cairyn from feeling lonely. She even moved her into my old room, thinking that it might help her to be surrounded by my things. She still has guilt because she thinks the move made it worse."

"How could she know that at the time?"

"That's what I said. Mom said she noticed Cairyn starting to withdraw, not wanting to come out of the room, not eating much. When she did come out, she looked horrible. Mom said she heard her leave sometimes late at night, but she never said where she went. Mom was too nice to ask her about it. She said she worried that she was cheating on me and Mom said she'd rather not know about it if she was. She loved Cairyn and knew she was hurting, so she didn't want to have to kick her out. So she let things go on, not knowing exactly what was up with her, until one day she found her passed out in the bathroom with a needle stuck in her arm."

"Oh my God."

"So Mom got her to the hospital, and when she woke up Mom told Cairyn that she would pay for her to get treatment if she was willing to do it. Cairyn agreed. The treatment seemed to work and she told Mom that she wanted to move back to our house, she thought it would be good for her, and Mom agreed. Two weeks later, she took more pills. I got the call the next day. That's how long it took for my mother to contact the Red Cross and the Red Cross to contact my First Shirt. I had just talked to Cairyn the day before to tell her that I couldn't come home for Christmas." Steve let go of Lou's hand to roll up the sleeve on her left arm. On her bicep was Cairyn's name, written in a pretty script, and below that a shattered rose and the date: *December 8, 2010.*

Lou reached over and traced the name and date very delicately, then leaned forward and put her arms around Steve's neck, placing a kiss there. "I'm sorry, baby. I'm so sorry."

Steve wrapped her arms around Lou, her breath coming in quick intakes. She held Lou tighter and buried her face in her hair. She whispered, "Lou, Lou…I think I'm falling in love with you."

Lou pulled back, cupping Steve's face with one hand, and said with a smile, "It's okay. I think I'm falling in love with you too." Then, very delicately, she kissed Steve on the lips.

Steve sighed. "What are we going to do about it, Boo Boo?"

Lou smiled. "Well, I think you can start by returning this *pic-a-nic* basket from where you stole it, then come to my house later."

"That sounds like an offer I can't refuse. Shall I wear a green tie?" Steve smiled mischievously.

"Only if you're going to wear a green hat to match."

"If I recall, Yogi didn't wear pants. I might get cold."

"I'll keep you warm." They kissed again, then Lou pulled away with a groan. "Okay, now look who's making a scene. I should stop. I have to still be able to go back to work today."

"Yeah, at least one of us should look respectable."

"Yet another role I get to play in this relationship." They stood up together and Lou put her arms around Steve again. "Thank you for sharing her with me."

"You're welcome. It was time."

After holding each other for some time, Lou helped Steve pack up and they said their good-byes. Then Lou went back to her building after Steve pulled out of the parking lot. Lou was glad Steve had told her about Cairyn, and now she understood what some of the tension had been about during dinner with Steve and her mom. She wanted to call Steve back and just put her arms around her and hold her for the rest of the day, letting her know everything was going to be okay. She sighed as she went up the stairs to her office, the impact of their shared admission of love hitting her, and she couldn't stop smiling.

Chapter Fourteen

L ou spent the rest of the afternoon doing what she referred to as distracted teaching. She just went through the motions in all her classes, vaguely aware when she was asked a question, then fumbling for the right answer. Her behavior was noticed by Melissa, the little redhead who always seemed the most concerned with her welfare.

"Are you all right, Dr. Silver?"

Lou gave her a small smile. "Yes, I'm fine, thank you for asking. Just something on my mind is all. Where was I?" She felt bad about teaching this way. They deserved her full attention, and she tried to always be present, but after her afternoon spent hearing about Steve's past, with the promise of intimacy later, she just couldn't muster up the appropriate amount of energy for teaching.

She somehow managed to get through the rest of her day without any major faux pas. Having a stage combat class in the afternoon helped. It forced her to stay focused on the task at hand in order to make sure no one got hurt.

When the day was over, she quickly locked up her office, making sure to grab her briefcase on the way out, though she doubted she would even open it tonight. She made her way down the hallway, nodding to a few students on the way by. Just as she reached the main doors and had her hand on the push bar, she heard her name being called. She hung her head and whispered, "So close." Then she turned with a fake smile on her face and said, "Hello, Charles."

"Don't forget, we have that meeting at five thirty."

"Meeting?"

"Only two weeks left in the semester. Finals are right around the corner." He smiled jovially at her, rocking back on his heels with his hands in his pockets.

Sure, he was in a good mood—his evening wasn't about to be ruined, Lou thought. She tried not to groan out loud. Those meetings were usually just a fat lot of wasted time, where they were reminded of university strategies, and how bad the current retention rate was. Very little business actually had to do with their department. But you had to stay awake and alert, because otherwise you were more than likely going to end up getting tasked with some time-wasting activity that the dean *volun-told* you for, no matter that you had no more time in your schedule.

"Isn't that later than usual?"

"Well, I had a conflict during our normal time, so the department meeting had to be rescheduled. I sent an email about the change on Friday. I figured you would have seen it by now." Charles looked confused.

Lou did remember seeing an email from the dean that morning, but with meeting Steve for lunch, and then the anticipation of later tonight, she had completely overlooked it and not even opened it. "I'm sorry, Charles. Teacher fail." She smiled at her own foolishness. "I didn't see it, and now I have this thing I have to go to that I can't get out of."

"What kind of thing?"

What kind of thing? She hadn't thought that far ahead. God, she was a horrible liar. "It's just…a thing," she said, hoping he'd drop the issue.

Still smiling, Charles asked, "Is it the same thing that brought you a picnic lunch?"

Her cheeks were burning. "Well, um…"

Charles laughed. "And when are you supposed to do this thing?"

She tried not to chuckle at his word choice. "I'm not sure exactly, but there are some things I have to do first."

"I'm sure, I'm sure. Well, can you spare me an hour? Besides, I might have a surprise for everyone." Charles grinned, as if he had secret knowledge to impart.

If the meeting was over by six thirty, that should still give her plenty of time to shower, she reasoned, but what about dinner? Were they having dinner? She wasn't sure, but she knew she wouldn't have enough time to cook something. "I guess I could."

"That's the spirit! Come on, we can go together."

Lou gave him her most sincere fake smile. Once seated at the conference table in the classroom they held their meetings in, she tried not to nod off. The meeting covered nothing of real interest and went until a quarter after seven. The homemade brownies Charles handed out to everyone, his promised surprise—carefully wrapped in cellophane, with red and green stringy ribbons hanging off them and a present tag affixed to the center with each of their names and little snowmen in the corners—were hardly compensation for the overlong meeting.

She ran out of the building, not bothering to make small talk with anyone on her way out. When she got to her car, she threw her bag, along with that damn brownie, into the back seat. During the meeting, Steve had texted to say she'd be there at eight, and it was now closing on seven thirty and she still had to get home and shower.

When she got home, she left everything in the back seat and hurried inside, throwing clothes off as she went, barely noticing the time, but fully aware she only had about fifteen minutes. She knew Steve would be on time. Punctual, reliable Steve would be ringing her doorbell right at the top of the hour, and Lou had to be ready. She jumped in the shower, quickly washing off the sweat from the day, realizing she wouldn't have time for her hair to dry. Maybe Steve would like the wet look, she hoped. She did a little essential maintenance with the razor, careful to take it slow for that part.

She was standing on her bath mat toweling off her hair when she heard it—the doorbell. She looked in the mirror and her eyes got wide with panic. Here she was, naked, a towel in her hand, her hair hanging wet and limp on her neck. "Fuck!" She wrapped the towel around her body, not even trying to put her hair up. What was the point? She scurried on damp feet to the front door, forgetting her glasses, she realized as she got to the living room. She opened the door to see Steve standing on her doorstep, hands crossed in front of herself and her smile of hello turning into one of surprise…and hunger.

"I think you're early." Lou smiled at her and cocked her head to the side.

"Uh, yeah. Bad habit. Would you like me to wait out here?" Steve indicated the porch.

"Oh my God, will you just get in here?" Lou laughed as she took Steve by the wrist and gently pulled her into the house. Once she was inside, Lou closed the door behind her and gave her a quick kiss on the lips. "Hi."

Steve put her arms around Lou's waist and kissed her back. "Hi, yourself. I suddenly feel overdressed."

"I'm sure I can get you another towel, if it would make you feel more comfortable."

"Why don't I just take yours?" Steve pulled Lou back to her and put her arms around her, her hands resting on Lou's ass.

Lou kissed her back passionately, but pulled back with a chuckle. "You seem to be obsessed with that body part."

"Just recognizing beauty when I see it." She brought her hands up to caress Lou's neck, moving the damp hair out of her way and placing her lips where her fingers had been.

Lou sighed in contentment and put her hands on Steve's backside, thinking, fair is fair. As Steve moved her lips up Lou's neck to her mouth, Lou pushed her body into Steve, then realized she was still wearing a damp towel and was probably getting

Steve's shirt all wet. She started to pull back some but Steve whimpered and asked, "Where are you going?"

"I just realized I was getting your shirt all wet."

Steve grinned. "Not just my shirt."

"Tsk-tsk, naughty, naughty."

"Nah, just being truthful. Tell me something…"

"Hmm?"

"Would it be terribly forward of me to say that I don't want to go through the preliminaries of dinner or having a drink and talking first? We've done all that. I just want to hold you close to me and feel you shake with pleasure underneath me." She kissed her again and Lou put her arms around her neck.

When she pulled away, she said, "Not so fast, soldier. I just might rock your world first."

"Well then, show me what you got, teacher."

Lou cocked an eyebrow and grinned, then grabbed Steve by the belt and maneuvered her until Steve was standing with her back to the door. Lou took a step back, raised her right hand and pointed her index finger, then extended her arm slowly, making contact with Steve's shoulder and pushing her against the door. She said with a smile, "This is called One-Finger Shooting Zen." Then she reached out and caressed Steve's breast, and Steve gave her an amused, yet surprised expression. Lou kissed her passionately.

Steve's arms went up and around her and kissed her back. "What was that move called?"

Lou grinned and said, "Lou takes control."

"Does she, now?"

"Oh, I would say so. You got a problem with that?"

Running her fingers along the top of Lou's towel, Steve smiled and said softly, "Ma'am, no ma'am."

"That's what I thought." Dropping her voice to a whisper, Lou asked, "Would you like me to remove the towel?"

Steve swallowed. "Yes, I would."

"Come on." Gently now, Lou grabbed Steve by the hand and

pulled her along to her bedroom. Once there, she went to the side of her bed and stopped and faced her. Lou dipped her head down, not in a gesture of submission or supplication but, rather, one of slyness and playfulness. When she looked back up at Steve, she said, "Are you ready?"

"Oh, yeah."

Very slowly, Lou took hold of her towel with both hands, unwrapped herself like a gift, and let the towel fall to the floor. Steve's breath picked up, and Lou closed the gap between them and put her fingers on the buttons of Steve's shirt.

Steve stood there, watching Lou work her buttons. Lou occasionally rewarded her patience with a kiss. Once the shirt was unbuttoned, Lou let it fall to the floor, and now Steve stood there in a white T-shirt and dress pants. Lou reached for Steve's belt. She had the leather belt undone and was holding on to both free ends now.

"I've waited a long time to feel you next to me," Lou said. "Is this what you want?"

"Oh yes." Steve knew this was what she'd been waiting for.

Using the belt, Lou pulled Steve to her and gave her a hard kiss. When Lou bit her lip it could have been accidental, but Steve knew it wasn't.

This felt good, so good, but it didn't seem right somehow. "Wait, wait."

"What's wrong?" Lou stopped abruptly and looked at Steve.

"It shouldn't be this way."

"What do you mean?"

"Oh, honey, take your time, I'm not going anywhere."

"Okay. You're right. We've waited this long—we should take our time and do it right."

"Yes." Steve reached out for Lou, feeling her warm skin. She almost went weak in the knees just at that first touch. Lou's lips had been warm and sensual, but her flesh...her flesh was smooth and toned and Steve wanted to just be against her. She went down on her knees and kissed Lou's flat stomach. Lou put her hands on Steve's shoulders and Steve held her hips. As Steve slowly kissed her way back up Lou's body, a low moan escaped Lou and her fingers moved to Steve's hair. Steve ran her tongue over the taut muscles, kissing and nibbling her way, worshipping her. Lou swayed against her as Steve continued her exploration of Lou's body with her lips.

Lou inhaled sharply when Steve ran her tongue over the flesh just above the beginning of her center. Lou's grip in Steve's hair became tighter. Steve stopped for just a moment and asked, "Would you like to sit back?"

Lou looked down and smiled. "No. Go on." She gently pushed Steve's head back where it was and Steve let her tongue find all the folds and creases until she reached Lou's clit and lightly ran her tongue over the tip, just barely there. Lou moaned deeper in her throat and Steve licked again, this time slower and over the whole tip, then very slowly did the same to Lou's lips and her slit, occasionally teasing the hole by darting her tongue in for a moment, then out again. Steve could feel Lou's grip on her tighten and her hips began to sway. Steve firmed her grip on Lou's hips as well but didn't stop what her tongue was doing.

"Oh God," Lou said. "I need to kiss you. Come up here, please."

Steve stood and took her in her arms. Lou's lips found Steve's, and this time, when she attacked Steve with passion, Steve just let it happen. Lou's tongue found hers and at the same time she began to feverishly pull at Steve's T-shirt. When she got it free of Steve's pants, she slid her hands under the shirt and pulled Steve closer. Her hands found Steve's breasts, and Lou lifted Steve's arms, pulled her shirt and bra off, and let them fall to the floor. Then she bent her head to Steve's chest and began to leave small kisses across it, and then she found her nipple and began to slowly suck on it. It was Steve's turn to inhale.

At first Lou was gentle with her. She ran her teeth along her nipple, just teasing, but then she started to slowly bite. "Yes, oh yes...more." She bit harder and a wordless moan escaped Steve this time. Lou slowly let go and started kissing up Steve's chest again until she got to her neck, where she sucked in her flesh, causing Steve to almost lose her balance.

Steve held on tighter until Lou finally pulled back and said, "This is not enough. I want to make love to you. I want to touch all of you. Come on, let's lie down."

Lou finished removing Steve's clothes, and then they lay down next to each other.

"This is what I want," Lou said. "I want to feel all of you. And I want to take my time."

And she did. Lou slowly ran her fingers over Steve. Up her arms, over her chest, around her breasts, up one leg and down the other. All so slowly. Steve's whole body came alive. When Lou finally entered her with two long, sure fingers, Steve was out of her mind with bliss. Steve sank her nails into Lou's shoulders and cried out, and when she finally shook with release, Lou came back up and put her lips to Steve's for a kiss that was just as gentle as her fingers had been. She whispered into her mouth, "I love you."

"I love you too."

Lou pulled the covers up over both of them and put her arms around Steve in a protective hug.

Exhausted, Steve mumbled, "I like it when you're in charge."

Lou laughed, then kissed Steve on the forehead.

Steve cuddled up against her and entwined their legs.

Steve moaned. She was no longer in Lou's embrace, having separated sometime in the night. She was hugging the edge of the bed, as she usually did when she slept, but now she was sweating as if she was running a fever. She was awake enough to know she needed something. Without opening her eyes, she reached out to the nightstand and fumbled around among the items on top, not finding it, knocking things to the floor in her search. She sat up in a panic and threw the covers off, hoping she could find it in the dark. She looked at the top of the unfamiliar nightstand, barely visible in the dark, and didn't see the familiar, comforting metallic presence of the chain. She felt her neck again to make sure she hadn't overlooked it while she slept, hoping against dwindling hope that it had just shifted while she slept to somewhere out of reach. But it wasn't there.

She got out of bed and crawled around until she found her clothes and began to frantically search through them in the dark. Lou stirred behind her, but she took little notice of it.

Lou sat up and asked sleepily, "Baby, what are you looking for?"

Distractedly, Steve said, "I've lost something." She found her pants and began to search the pockets, even though there was no way it could have worked its way into one of them on its own.

"Of course, but what, exactly, are you looking for?"

"My chain."

"Your chain? Oh, the Capricorn pendant. Come back to bed— we'll look for it in the morning. It's gotta be here somewhere."

Lou reached across the bed and turned on the light on her nightstand and could see Steve clearly for the first time. She was kneeling on the floor, naked, a look of pure panic on her face.

"I need it. I need it now. I won't be able to sleep without it."

Lou got out of bed, joined Steve on her knees, and put her hand on Steve's shoulder, the one with the tattoo. Very calmly, she asked, "Baby, why is it so important to you?"

Steve finished with the pants and threw them aside, then picked up her outer shirt and began doing the same thing with that. Without looking at Lou, she replied, "Because it was hers."

"Oh," Lou said quietly. Then she removed her hand from Steve's shoulder and repeated, "It's here somewhere." She began a slower, more methodical search of Steve's clothing, as well as the floor, making sure she did not miss anything. She saw an unfamiliar metallic glint coming from under the bed and reached her hand underneath until she found the offending object and retrieved it. She pulled it out from under the bed and held it out to Steve. "Here it is."

Steve turned around, her eyes huge, and said, "You found it? Oh, thank God." She snatched it from Lou's outstretched hand and held it to her lips and kissed it, then held it to her chest with her eyes closed for a moment. She exhaled, now visibly calmer, and put the necklace on. Once it was on, her breathing slowed down and she sighed. She turned to Lou and said, "Thank you for finding it."

"Of course." Lou smiled and put her hand on Steve's shoulder again, then reached over and kissed her on the cheek. "Come on, let's go back to bed." She moved her hand to the middle of Steve's back.

"Yeah, okay." As they were climbing back into bed, Steve noticed Lou's glasses on the floor, picked them up, and put them back on the nightstand. "Oh, crap, I'm sorry. I didn't mean to knock those off."

"It's all right, no harm done. Come here." Lou lay back on her pillows with her arms open.

Steve crawled into her embrace and let Lou put her arms around her and hold her to her chest. Steve put her arm around Lou's waist and sighed against her. "Why are you so nice?"

Lou chuckled. "Because I love you."

"That simple?"

"Yep."

"Amazing."

"What's amazing?"

Steve took her head off Lou's chest long enough to look her in the eyes. "You are. You're a strong woman to be able to handle all this."

Lou gently pushed Steve's head back onto her chest, but not before kissing her on the forehead. "I'm not that strong."

"Yeah, you are. A lot of women would be thrown by…my past, or be jealous of her or something."

"I'm not most women. What point would there be in being

jealous of a troubled young woman who's no longer walking this earth? Besides, she's a part of you and I love you. That means taking all of this and helping you with it, in whatever way I can." Lou squeezed her tighter and smoothed her hair.

"That's why I say you're strong. That, and being able to deal with your own stuff too."

"Some days are better than others."

"I think you've dealt with your stuff better than I have. It took me years to stop having full-on panic attacks. Now I just have mild freak-out moments, but I've developed ways to get over them."

"The necklace?"

"Yeah."

"You're wrong. I haven't really dealt with anything—I just shove it away and try to forget about it. So, no, I'm not strong. I'm just a good actress."

Steve tightened her grip around Lou's waist and kissed her chest. "Coulda fooled me."

Lou whispered, "I know. Go to sleep now, love. Morning will be here before you know it." Lou kissed her again, then snuggled down a little farther so they were face to face. Steve draped an arm over her and Lou closed her eyes and slowly, meditatively, ran her fingers over Steve's back and arms, drawing lazy circles and shapeless shapes, and fell asleep with Steve's face burrowed into her shoulder.

Chapter Fifteen

The next morning, Lou woke up first to find herself on her back, with Steve draped across her stomach, the covers kicked aside, and only a thin sheet covering them. She chuckled. If this was indicative of how Steve slept on a regular basis, they were going to have a struggle over sleeping arrangements. Lou was a snuggler from way back, always preferring to pull the covers all the way up to her chin, as long as it wasn't too hot in the house. Speaking of which, she could feel the heat coming from Steve as she slept, which explained why the covers were currently half hanging off the bed. Snuggling in covers was one thing, but dealing with Steve's natural body heat something else. She groaned as she came more awake. "Baby, I love you, but for the love of God, get off me, you're hot." She laughed to hopefully quell any concern from Steve that she just didn't want her to touch her.

Steve came awake slowly, groaned too, then rolled off Lou, but not before kissing her on the stomach on the way by. She smiled. "I know I'm hot. This isn't news."

Lou lightly smacked her on the chest. "Morning ego check."

"I've checked—I've got one."

"I've noticed."

"Well, sometimes we have to sing our own praises."

Lou rolled over on her elbow, then reached up and gave Steve a quick kiss. "You want me to sing your praises? Go make me a pot of coffee. Please. Then I will sing your praises all over the land."

"What would you do if I also made you breakfast?" Steve brushed a curl off Lou's forehead and kissed her back.

Lou smiled. "Mm, let's see, if you make me coffee *and* breakfast? Then I will sing your praises on a full stomach."

Chuckling, Steve asked, "So what can I get you?"

"Got your pad ready?"

Steve mimed pulling out a waiter's pad and pen and paused with one hand in the air, as if she was waiting for Lou's order. "I'm ready."

"Okay, I would like coffee strong enough to clean the rust off a '57 Buick, with three scrambled eggs in butter, and a piece of whole wheat toast. Oh, and a real morning kiss." She grinned.

Steve pretended to throw the pad over her shoulder and took Lou in her arms and gave her a kiss, a kiss almost worth being late to work for. But Lou pushed her away after a few minutes and said, "I think we need to stop that for now so I can go take a shower and you can rustle up some breakfast."

"Rustle up? Who do I look like, a cowhand?"

Lou pretended to consider the question. "Hmm, not really. More like G.I. Joe's younger sister who wanted to follow in her brother's footsteps." Lou laughed and mussed Steve's hair.

"Kid sister? Kid sister!" She reached out to tickle Lou, but Lou squealed and scurried out of the other side of the bed.

She ran out the door to the bathroom, Steve chasing her the whole way, but Lou got there first and closed the door behind her. She opened it momentarily to say, "At least G.I. Jane has a nice butt." Then she closed the door again among her giggles.

She didn't lock it, but Steve didn't try to open it. Instead she said, loud enough to be heard through the door, "Thank you. My ego and I are going to get dressed now, and then make breakfast."

Lou opened the door and called out to Steve, who was walking out of the bedroom. "You're not good with signals, are you?"

"What are you talking about?"

"I left the door unlocked for a reason."

"Oh." Steve smiled shyly and Lou crooked her finger and Steve obeyed. When she reached her, she took Lou into her arms, moaning as their mouths met again, and Lou pushed her up against the sink. "What about breakfast?" Steve managed to ask.

"Oh, I'll be having something." Then Lou kissed her way down Steve's body, until she reached her center. Now on her knees, she let her tongue explore, while Steve gripped the countertop.

"Oh God. Oh yes…yeah. Mm." Steve put one hand on Lou's head and ran her fingers through her hair, while she thrust her own head back and closed her eyes. The moan was now just a sound deep in her throat, with no actual words. When her moment of bliss came, her body went rigid for a moment, then began to shake and her knees started to buckle. Lou pulled away and stood and put her arms around her as Steve's body shook with orgasm, and then Lou held Steve as she collapsed against her. Steve wrapped her arms around Lou's waist and Lou placed little kisses on Steve's neck.

Lou whispered, "I love you."

Steve put a small kiss on Lou's shoulder and whispered, "I love you too."

❖

Steve went to the kitchen to make Lou the promised coffee, while Lou was dressing after their shower, where Steve had been able to return the favor. When Steve walked into the kitchen, she noticed it was the neatest room in the house. There were no dirty dishes in the sink, and the floors and counters were spotless. Steve smiled. Either the kitchen was so clean because it was just the one room Lou cared about the most, since even the messiest people had one room they kept spotless, or it was because Lou didn't cook. Steve opened the fridge to retrieve the breakfast supplies and saw the same thing in there. She retrieved the items she needed and set them on the counter next to the stove, then went in search of the coffee. Lou had an expensive-looking coffeepot that was somewhat intimidating to Steve. Steve's coffeepot's most technical features were that she could program it to make coffee in the morning and that it automatically shut itself off. Lou's machine had several buttons Steve wasn't even sure what they did. She was able to get the coffee and water in the machine, and she found the brew button, but she wasn't sure how to make the coffee stronger. She knew some coffeepots had that capability.

She was still studying the front of the machine when Lou walked in. "If you push that button three times, it becomes industrial strength rust remover. Just the way I like it." Lou smiled to see her, standing in front of the machine with her hands on her hips, looking over the buttons like she was trying to decipher hieroglyphics. She walked up behind Steve and purposely pushed against her, then leaned around her and pushed the button. Then she snaked her arms around Steve's waist and kissed her on the back of the neck.

"So that's where it is. Thank you." Steve leaned into her, then turned her head slightly to kiss Lou on the lips.

"You're welcome." Lou released her and Steve began making breakfast again. While Steve cooked, Lou set the table and retrieved coffee cups and placed them near the coffeepot, then put bread in the toaster. She smiled at Steve's back, thinking how natural this seemed, them working together in the kitchen. It was only their first morning. It wasn't supposed to feel this comfortable this soon, was it? Weren't they supposed to take months to get this familiar with each other? Then she shook her head, realizing she was starting to analyze it to death, and she didn't want to do that. Instead, she went to the fridge for the blackberry preserves she knew she still had from the last time she had gone to the farmers' market, back before school had started for the semester. Retrieving the jar, she asked, "What would you like on your toast? I have three kinds of jelly." She held aloft the blackberry preserves as if for emphasis.

Steve took the jar from her and read the label. "That's preserves. You shouldn't call it jelly." Then she grinned.

Lou did too. "I remember that commercial. Cute, but it doesn't answer my question."

"Fine. Do you have apricot?"

"Do I have apricot?" Lou asked, in the manner of an overenthusiastic salesman, then changed her tone to one of actual inquiry, "Wait, *do* I have apricot?" She moved bottles around in the fridge until she came up with the right one. "It appears that I do have apricot." She held it up for Steve to see, and Steve leaned over and planted a kiss on her cheek.

"You are too cute."

"Then I will work on my ugly face." She screwed up her face, then asked, "How's this?"

"Nope, still cute. I think it might be a terminal problem." Steve scooped scrambled eggs onto their plates, then turned around to quickly make their toast while Lou got each of them a cup of coffee. She was enjoying being in the kitchen with Lou. It seemed homey and definitely something she could get used to.

They sat down to eat and were enjoying their meal, exchanging pleasantries. Steve started to think back to her little freak-out earlier that morning. She had started calling those moments little freak-outs because they never became full-blown panic attacks like they used to, back before she learned to control them. But she hadn't done it without help. Once she pushed her plate aside and sat back to finish her coffee, she looked across the table at Lou and remembered something from the night before. She looked at her with concern and asked, "What did you mean earlier when you said that you're a good actress?"

Lou looked up. "What? When did I say that?"

"This morning, after I got up to find my necklace. After we had climbed back into bed. You said it right before I fell back asleep. What'd you mean by it?"

"Oh." She remembered the conversation now. They had been talking about their separate baggage. "Well, I guess…just that my way of dealing with my issues is to ignore them. Act like everything's okay. Because I can't change it and it's over now, so why dwell on it?" She shrugged as if it was no big deal.

"But if you have to act, then it's not over. It obviously still troubles you. And just because the abuse has stopped doesn't mean it's over." Steve reached over and took Lou's hand.

Lou gave her a small smile. "Steve, my father's dead. It's over. Now hand me your plate." She reached out her hand, but Steve just sat there and looked at her. "Can I have your plate, please?"

Steve handed her plate over but said nothing.

Lou stood up and took the plates to the sink, then immediately started to rinse them off, not saying a word. She could tell the mood in the room had greatly shifted.

Finally, Steve stood a few feet behind her. Very gently, she said, "Lou, don't shut down and don't shut me out."

Lou finished washing a plate and put it in the drainer to dry. She said flatly, "I'm not shutting you out. I'm just doing the dishes."

Steve sighed. "Lou, I was just going to say that I think you might want to talk to someone about your past, maybe work through it."

Lou went still a moment, then set the dishes she was washing back in the sink. She shut the faucet off, then turned around to face Steve, wiping her hands on the back of her pants. "Are you saying I need therapy?"

"Well, I think it would—"

"Help me?" Lou cut her off. "Do you really think it would help me to relive all that stuff again? To remember all the times he hit me? All the things he called me? It took me years to stop thinking about it all the time. I couldn't sleep through the night without panic for five years after he left. Took me longer to stop looking over my shoulder, or worrying about not cleaning the kitchen up to his standards. Do you know what would happen if I left food on a fork or let food spill over in the microwave and didn't wipe it up?"

"Oh, honey…" Steve reached out for her, but Lou backed away.

"No. I can't go through that again. I finally like my life the way it is. I'm finally free of him."

"Are you?"

"Louis Wayne Silver died on April 19, 2005. I'd say that's pretty fucking final." Lou cleared her throat. When she spoke again, it was with false cheer. "Now we need to get out of here. There's this place they pay me to go to every day, so it'd probably be a good idea if I showed up. You too, trainer." She smiled, then moved to leave the room, but not without swatting Steve's butt on the way by.

Steve gave her a small smile. "Lou?"

Lou turned to look at her. "Yes?"

Several things came to Steve's mind to say, but she feared Lou would shut her out again, or worse, become angry at her, so she thought better of it, not wanting to fight. Instead, she walked up to Lou and put her arms around her and kissed her on the cheek. She whispered, "Nothing, I just wanted to say I love you."

Lou hugged her back. "That's not nothing. That's everything. And I love you too." Lou pecked Steve on the lips, then stepped out of the embrace. "Come on, we need to go do our thing. Well, not *that* thing—the thing we get paid to do."

Steve chuckled, but her heart really wasn't in it. She let Lou set the tone for now, telling herself that this would not be the last time she would bring Lou's past up.

Chapter Sixteen

When Lou got to campus, she went to her office, but only long enough to drop off her bag and the coffee mug Steve sent her to work with. Then she left and went somewhere she had never been to before. She walked across campus until she came to the back corner of the property, skirting the edge of the biggest parking lot on campus, which serviced three dorms, the football field, and the gym. It was to the gym she went now. The athletics office was just to the left of the door and Lou could see a blond student inside wearing a purple and gold school hoodie, her head bent over a book. She looked up when Lou approached the glass and smiled.

The girl opened the sliding window and asked, "Hi. How can I help you?"

Lou returned her smile. "Yes, hello, I'm Dr. Silver, a professor on campus. I was just wondering if I could work out here. Do I need to pay a fee or anything?"

"Nope, it's a job perk. The only ones who have to pay are staff and alumni. The gym is down this hallway, to the right. You'll see the locker rooms along the way. Make yourself at home. Oh, but you do need to flash me your ID."

"Yes, of course." Lou showed the young woman her campus ID, then followed her instructions to find the locker room. She quickly staked out a spot and changed into her workout clothes, stashing her gym bag in a locker and using the lock that she always kept in the bag. Then she headed out to the gym.

The room she walked into a moment later was huge. All the equipment was state of the art, some of which Lou was unfamiliar with—she wasn't always sure what part of the body a machine worked out. It was clear the athletic department was well funded and could afford to buy nothing but the best. Lou walked around the gym, taking a silent inventory and looking for the gear she had come there for. She passed all the various cardio machines, the treadmills, ellipticals, the StairMasters. Behind them were the individual machines people could use to work out different muscle groups, each one targeting a specific area of the body. It all seemed so artificial to Lou. She preferred the older methods, the dumbbells and bench press, calisthenics. Sometimes she used the Universal, but only because it offered more resistance than the free weights. Her sifu had once jokingly called her a fitness Luddite, and she couldn't refute the charge. She had laughed. "If I ever had to train to fight a Russian, I would much rather do it in a log cabin, using logs as weights and running up the side of a mountain," she had joked, referencing one of the *Rocky* movies.

Finally at the back of the gym she found what she had come for: the heavy bag. On the wall next to it were gloves. She found a pair that fit her well enough and put them on, then set her stance, focused on the spot on the bag she wanted to shoot for, then started hitting. She started with light jabs at first, without much energy behind them, then, after a few punches, put more power behind them and just kept hitting the bag, over and over, not sure how long, just until she started to feel it in her shoulder and her hair worked its way loose from her clip. She could feel the sweat dripping down her back and she wiped it from her brow using her sleeve, trying to cut it off at the pass before it reached her eyes. Panting, she pulled off the gloves and hung them back on the wall, only then realizing she had forgotten her water bottle. She had noticed a water fountain when she had walked in, so she made her way over to it before heading back to the locker room.

Normally when she had something to work through, she went to the Wushuguan and worked out there, but now Steve was there and she didn't want her to know that the morning's conversation had gotten to her as much as it had. She knew Steve only brought up the idea of therapy because she loved her, but she hated the very idea of it. She didn't need it anyway, she thought. She was mostly over the past. The man was dead, her body had long since healed, and she was no longer afraid. What was there to work out? Therapy was just one of those things, like getting married and having children, that once other people did it, they tried to get all their friends to do it too. Not everyone needed to sit on a couch and discuss their feelings all day with someone who was getting paid to listen to other people's problems, probably while avoiding their own. Who needed it? It was self-indulgent navel-gazing and Lou didn't have time for it. Her issues, what was left of them, weren't so bad that a good round with the heavy bag, or a full body workout in general, couldn't fix them. She just hoped Steve would drop it.

When she got back to the locker room she noticed there was a student in the same alcove of lockers where she had stashed her clothes. She walked past the student, who had her back to her, over to her locker and took out her bag. She had her T-shirt off and was retrieving her shirt for the day. She wasn't nearly sweaty enough to warrant showering, as she kinda hated showering at the gym anyway. The student turned around and immediately blushed to see Lou standing there in her sports bra.

"Um, hi, Dr. Silver. Haven't seen you in here before."

Lou saw the girl's distress and bit back a smile as she quickly put her regular shirt back on. "Hey, Melissa. Yeah, this is my first time here. Thought I'd check the place out. You work out here?"

Melissa gave her a nervous smile, then ducked her head. "Yeah. It's free for students."

Lou grinned. "Yeah, for me too. It's a nice perk. I'll have to come back more often. See you in class later." Lou beat a hasty retreat, lest she embarrass the girl further, thinking about how traumatized she would have been to turn around to see one of her teachers standing behind her, half naked. Poor girl, Lou thought. Class that afternoon was going to be interesting.

❖

As predicted, class that afternoon with Melissa was a bit awkward, with the girl avoiding eye contact as much as possible. Once, when Lou came up to her to demonstrate a parry move and touched Melissa's wrist to put it in the proper position, the girl blushed so deeply, it made Lou falter in her demonstration. *That'll be the last time I work out on campus, if this is what comes of it.* She wondered why the girl would react that way—she'd been less uncovered than she would have been in a swimming pool, after all.

Later, as she and Steve were sitting around Lou's kitchen table having dinner, Steve laughed at the gym story and said, "I'm surprised you don't see it. I can see it, and I've never met the poor girl."

"What are you talking about?" At first, she wasn't going to tell Steve she had gone to work out on campus, considering why she had done so, but she didn't want to start their relationship out by lying about such an insignificant little thing. Steve had looked thoughtful when she'd mentioned it but hadn't questioned her choice.

"Baby, she's got a crush on you, or at the very least, she thinks you're hot. She's been able to control her thoughts about that in class, until she saw you naked. I understand her problem. I can't stop blushing around you either." Steve took Lou's hand, then leaned over and placed a small kiss on her lips before sitting back and smiling at her.

"I wasn't *naked*. You really think that's it?"

"I do. Is that so hard to believe?"

Lou shrugged. "I don't know, just not used to it, I guess."

"Oh, please," Steve scoffed.

"What?"

"What about that other soldier in your life? She was hot for you. You got girls twenty years younger than you falling at your feet and you still don't know how awesome you are."

Now it was Lou's turn to get all hot and bothered. She mumbled, "I should have never told you about her."

Steve laughed. "I thought it was sweet. Makes me realize I'm going to have to up my game, though, if I want to keep you. Now that you know you have options, what'll you need me for?" She grinned, then laughed when Lou threw her napkin at her.

"Well, where have all those options been the last couple of years before you came along?"

"What do you mean?"

"I mean in the last two years, since my last relationship, no one has noticed my awesomeness. But now, besides you, I have two girls I could have given birth to who seem to have noticed. Where were those sweet young things when I was putting up profiles on dating sites and lamenting the state of lesbian dating?" Lou was laughing at herself and it felt good.

Steve seemed amused also and laughed with her, but after a moment she looked at Lou shrewdly and said, "Oh, they were probably still there, but I doubt you saw them."

"What do you mean?"

"What I mean is I just don't think they were on your radar because they're not who you were looking for. Of course, I wasn't exactly what you were looking for either, but I was just persistent." Steve winked at her.

"So are you saying they were there the whole time, but because I was looking for some other type of woman, I didn't even see them? That I was blind to them?"

"That's *exactly* what I'm saying." Steve used her fork for emphasis to gesture at Lou.

Lou shook her head. "I just don't buy it. Steve, I was mostly happy being single, but I was lonely sometimes too. I *wanted* a girlfriend. I was *hoping* for a girlfriend. I don't think I would have overlooked girls who were falling at my feet."

"Maybe. But you almost overlooked me. I had to get my mother to introduce us. When I tried it on my own, you literally walked right past me."

"Steve, the first time I ever saw you was when your mother introduced me to you. And I talked to you then. And I was charmed by you. And I still am." Lou gave Steve the warmest of smiles.

Steve sat back and folded her arms over her chest and smiled. "I knew you didn't see me."

"Care to tell me what you're talking about?"

"I'd been coming to pick my mother up every Saturday for a month. I would wait inside the front door, by the display case. I saw you walk by that first day, and I smiled at you and said hi, but you kept walking. Didn't see me. I thought, well maybe she's just in a hurry, she'll see me next time. The next week, same thing. So the third week I thought I would try something more than hello, and so that time when you walked by, I tried to get your attention a different way. I was dressed in my black boots, snug blue jeans, an Army T-shirt—I was looking fierce." They exchanged a smile. "You *did* look at me that time, but the look you gave me could have melted stone."

Lou looked horrified at the thought. "I was rude to you?"

"Well, you didn't say anything, so you weren't rude in that sense, but you looked at me like I was a scrub hanging out of my best friend's car, and I was definitely not going to get any love from you." Steve shrugged it off.

Lou did too, but Steve could tell it bothered her to think she had been mean. "I'm so sorry. I don't know why I would have acted that way."

"No biggie. I just figured you either didn't like butches, and I was looking very butch that day, or it was my shirt. You did kinda look at my shirt before you looked at my face."

Looking sheepish, Lou admitted, "It was probably both. The Army thing for obvious reasons, and the butch thing…I'm not sure why, exactly. I mean, I used to tell myself that I just wasn't attracted to butches, but that is patently false. I've always known that. I think it had more to do with needing to feel like I was the masculine one in a relationship, so I needed my counterpart."

Steve rolled her eyes at Lou's comment.

"And I see that look," Lou continued. "I know I'm not that masculine, but I'm not that feminine either."

"Nope, you're just Lou. And there's nothing wrong with that." Steve smiled and they shared another kiss.

"Thank you." Lou sighed and sat back in her chair with a thoughtful expression on her face. "Plus, if I'm being truthful, butches have always been about strength and independence to me, and *Step aside, little lady*. I didn't want to deal with that. I give up my independence for no one."

"Misogynists, you mean?"

"Seems so harsh, but yeah, I guess."

"Some butches are—not because they're butch, but because they're people with a skewed view of the world. And they're assholes. But as you can see, most of us just want to find a nice woman to romance and charm and to treat her like the precious, badass creature she is, and just love her to pieces." Steve smiled, then felt self-conscious. "And when push comes to shove, we are big cream puffs who have to ask our mothers to help us get a girl's attention sometimes."

Lou laughed, then reached over and cupped Steve's face in her hands. "Well, you have my attention now. And I think we should make up for lost time." She cocked her head toward the bedroom, and then she kissed Steve so long and so passionately, it brought out a moan. Lou broke off the kiss and leaned back again. "Come on, cream puff, show me what you got." She took Steve's hand, stood up from the table, and started walking through the house, to her room, pulling Steve behind.

CHAPTER SEVENTEEN

The next morning, Lou was in her office trying to get through her emails quickly, so she could spend the rest of the morning grading the final papers that had come in early from some of her eager students. She couldn't blame them for wanting to get through some of their work early, as most had several essays to do, and letting them all pile up until the last minute was not the best strategy. She had done the same thing herself when she'd been in college. She never missed a deadline, never asked for an extension. She knew she was there to study, not to party. She had never understood why so many of her classmates didn't see it that way. She had been lucky to fall in with a group of geeks her freshman year who all felt the same way she did, and no one made fun of her for begging off group activities so she could spend the weekend roaming the library or hunched at her desk, not moving unless one dire need or the other made itself known.

She did have fun with her friends, often doing things like playing D&D or having Monty Python marathons hosted by Jim, the only member of the group who had all the movies and would often say lines along with the actors, knew the words to all the songs, and would sing them at top volume. She had been lucky to find those irregulars, as they allowed her to finally be more herself. They had accepted her coming out with ease, even when it surprised them. She had been nervous to come out to them at first and had come out to her best friend, Dave, initially.

His reaction surprised her the most. "So? You want a cookie?" It had left her speechless. She had built up this whole dramatic scenario in her head, and when he didn't give her that, she had no idea how to respond to his blatant acceptance. Finally, after several moments, she realized that his reaction was the right one—coming out should be treated as no big deal. The rest of her friends had reacted in similar ways, not one of them rejecting her. Her male friends even began to lightly tease her. Her friend Brad would sometimes ask her whether she was having any luck with the ladies, and they'd commiserate about their dating woes.

Ah, dating in college…She had noticed a lot of attractive young women on campus, but it didn't seem like they noticed her. When she did find someone to date, it was someone her roommate had introduced her to, a friend of hers from high school who lived several hours away from their campus. They made it work for a couple of years, with one or the other of them driving out for a stolen weekend of passion or a week or two over Christmas break. Steve's comments from the night before came back to her. She wondered if there actually *had* been women who had noticed her back then on campus, but she hadn't noticed them because they hadn't fit the ideal of what she thought she was looking for, and she had completely dismissed them. Could Steve be right? Were there women who didn't even register on her radar? God, if there were, she hoped she hadn't been rude to them the way she had been rude and dismissive to Steve. The encounters Steve described, about trying to get Lou's attention…Lou felt horrible about that. She always tried to treat everyone with kindness.

She picked up her phone and sent a quick message to Steve: *You are so kind and gentle and I don't deserve you. I love you.* She set the phone back on her desk and blinked and tried to refocus on the screen in front of her. She had just opened an email from a student with the subject line *Final Paper* when there was a knock on her door. It wasn't time for her office hours yet and she was hoping to get some work done, but it wasn't in her nature to ignore the knock, even when she would much rather be doing something else. She hollered out, "Come in."

The door opened and a hand shot through first holding a paper cup from her favorite coffee shop, and Lou smiled. "Come in, Bill."

Bill poked his head around the door, opening it more, and asked, "How'd you know it was me?"

"Because coffee rarely knocks on my door unassisted. And since Rachel graduated, you're the only coffee fairy I have." She winked at him and accepted the cup with her thanks.

Closing the door behind him, he replied, "I'm the only coffee fairy you know who's actually a fairy." He took the seat next to her desk and sipped his coffee.

Lou sat back in her chair and took off the lid, setting it on her desk. "I've been meaning to ask, and I'm sure you can speak for everyone in your tribe. Why fairy?" She sipped her coffee, made the way she liked it.

Bill seemed to contemplate the question. "I could ask you the same question. Why dyke?"

"That *is* a good question. Whose idea was it to pick a label that referenced a structure that retains water? Always thought that was rude."

"Hmm, but accurate." Lou scoffed and threw her lid at him. He laughed and dodged it.

Lou said, "As least fairy refers to ethereal creatures who are beautiful and spread glitter everywhere and I think I just figured that one out." They laughed together again, but then Lou grew thoughtful.

Bill took a sip of his coffee and looked over at her. "Something troubling you, princess?"

"I should kick you out of my office for slander. I am not a princess. I rescue princesses, thank you very much."

"Thank God you don't have to do that anymore. Sgt. Hottie seems capable of taking care of herself."

"True. I might have to hang up my sword and stable my white horse if this keeps up."

"Quit dodging my question and tell me what's on your mind."

"You are annoyingly persistent."

"That's what it says on my résumé. Come on, tell me."

Lou sighed. "I don't know, just something Steve said last night that I can't stop thinking about."

"What'd she say?"

Instead of answering, Lou asked, "Bill, do you think I overlook women who don't fit my ideal?"

"Yes."

"Wow, that was quick. Are you sure you don't want to think about it for a minute?"

"Don't need to."

"Then care to explain?"

"Simple, sweetie. Just in the short time I've known you, I've seen you walk by several women who were giving you the eye, and you didn't even register their existence. These women could have been plastic plants, for all the notice you took of them." Bill crossed his legs out in front of him and gave her a matter-of-fact look.

Lou looked abashed. "Did these women have anything in common?"

"How would I know? It's not like I stopped and had a conversation with them."

"I mean, were they like Steve?"

"Oh, I see what you mean. Were they more masculine of center, as the kids are saying these days?" Lou nodded. "Yeah, I guess they were, now that you mention it. Why, does that bother you?"

"The thought that I may have been rude to them, even unconsciously, bothers me. The thought that I might have missed out on knowing some great women because I was caught up with the ideal I had in my head of the perfect woman, that bothers me."

"Don't worry about it. I'm sure it wasn't that big a deal to them. People are rejected every day—it's something we all have to deal with. And I'm sure you weren't rude to them. You don't have it in you to be rude. How can you be rude to someone you don't see?"

He hadn't meant the words to sting, but they did. She tried not to wince at their implications. "Just something I need to be more mindful of in the future, I guess. Anyway, that's enough of this maudlin crap, what's up with you? And why did you bring me coffee? Not that I am protesting in the slightest." She grinned at him as she took another sip.

"Well, returning the favor, for one. Also, to see you. I miss you, pet."

Lou scrutinized him. "What's with the cutesy nicknames? Are you trying to butter me up for something?"

Bill put his hand to his chest and mocked looking shocked. "You question my motives? I'm appalled. Oh!" Then he dramatically tossed his head to the side as if he couldn't bear to look at her.

Lou snorted. "You're such a drama queen."

Bill turned back around with a grin. "That's what it says on the nameplate on my desk under my name." Bill took a sip of coffee and an innocent look came over him. "Also, I was wondering if you could proctor one of my finals for me. My final final of the semester."

"I *knew* there was something. Don't you have grad assistants for that?"

"No, they cut the funding, remember?"

"How would I know that? Us untenured folks don't have the privilege of grad assistants anyway. That's for you posh people."

"Well, what's the use of being posh when you have to do

your own grunt work? I have plenty of suck-up seniors who I could ask, but I'd rather have a professor do it. And I trust you."

"Why are you asking this, anyway? What are you going to be doing instead?"

Bill mumbled into his coffee cup. "Spend a week in Key West."

Lou's mouth fell open. "That's why you need a proctor?" He nodded. Lou chuckled and shook her head in amusement. "Oh, how the posh live. What time is the exam?" she asked with a gesture of defeat.

He just grinned in triumph.

She pointed an accusing finger at him. "I never said I would do it, so don't get ahead of yourself."

"Okay." He gave her the information she asked for, then put his hands to his chest as if in prayer, although the posture was awkward, since he still held his coffee cup. "Please?"

Lou sighed as if it was a major imposition, even though it really wasn't that hard to sit in a room babysitting undergrads. She could bring her laptop and get some grading done. She would have two hours in a quiet room, where no one would be knocking on her door and calling her, and she could concentrate on what she was doing. One thing did occur to her, however. "Why don't you just do a take-home test?"

"If they were upperclassmen or grad students I would, but it's freshmen. Must keep up the tradition of torturing them, so that when they're upperclassmen and are given the gift of a take-home final, they will appreciate it."

"Ah yes, of course. Torturing young people is one of the main reasons I took this job," she joked.

"Exactly. Don't be surprised if some leave crying. Happens every year."

"I'll bring a box of tissues. Fine. Have fun, you slacker."

"If only I had a magic wand to sprinkle you with magic fairy dust right now, I would."

"I'd rather you didn't. Glitter is forever."

"That's why it's magical." Bill mimed jazz hands and Lou just shook her head.

After Bill left, a text came in from Steve: *Just getting this, was with a client. No, I'm not. You are the epitome of kindness and I love you so much. You are a goddess.*

Lou was so moved. Her cheeks grew warm, and she was glad she was alone. She sighed contentedly and sent back the biggest smile she could text.

Chapter Eighteen

On Saturday, Steve drove her mother home after her lesson with Lou, but not before kissing Lou good-bye and making plans for later. Her mother was in a great mood, as she usually was after her time with Lou. She said the workout energized her, and that was easy to believe.

"I hope you have invited her over for Christmas. She's a part of this family now and it's time she realized it. Poor thing, doesn't have a family of her own anymore."

Her mother only knew that Lou's parents were both gone, but nothing about her abusive childhood. Steve figured she would find out in time, but it wasn't her story to tell. Steve looked at her mother now and smiled. "She's really a part of the family now?"

Her mother smacked Steve's knee good-naturedly. "Don't be daft—you know she is."

"Once you're an Adams..." Steve broke off in the same place her father would have, waiting for her mother to respond.

She played her part with a smile. "You're always an Adams. Exactly. I know you haven't married her yet, but all things in time," her mother declared knowingly.

"Married? Mother, we haven't even been dating that long."

"When it's right, it's right. How long does it really take to know you've met the one you want to spend the rest of your life with?"

Steve tightened her grip on the steering wheel. With Cairyn, she had known after that first kiss. That was all it took. With Lou, it had kind of snuck up on her. It had happened so gradually, she wasn't sure of the exact moment. But her mother was right—sometimes you just knew. Instead of dwelling on all that, Steve asked, "When did you know you were going to marry Dad? And if you say *When I got pregnant* I will stop this car right now and leave you on the side of the road."

"Such a way to talk to an old lady. Were you raised by wolves?"

"Close. Hippies, apparently."

"Humph. Anyway, to answer your question, I knew I wanted to marry your father the first time I saw him on campus. He was standing in the middle of a group of people on the quad, giving a speech against the war. Oh, he was so passionate and he spoke so well that it brought tears to my eyes. I didn't know about your uncle John yet, the reason he was so passionate."

"I forget about Uncle John sometimes. MIA, right?"

"Yes. It broke your father's heart, but it gave him a cause, and he fought diligently for it. I took one look at him, standing there in his bell-bottoms, with his long hair, and I thought he was so handsome. I knew I wanted to know him, and it struck me out of nowhere—that's the man I'm going to marry. I don't know where it came from. Before that, marriage was not something I thought too much about, other than to dismiss it as something I didn't want to do for a long, long time. But I knew someday that man would be the father of my children, and we would grow old on the porch together. I guess I was half right." Her mother dabbed at the corners of her eyes and turned to look out the window.

Steve reached over and patted her on the leg. She tried to make her mother laugh. "I can't imagine Dad with long hair. I don't even remember him having hair."

Steve's attempt to divert the heavy emotions her mother's story evoked worked and her mother laughed. "I know. He started losing it when you were a baby and had a bare dome by the time you were in junior high. He used to say marriage and fatherhood were rough." Lorraine laughed again.

"Mom, was he…was he…was he really proud of me when I joined the Army?"

"Didn't I tell you he was? He didn't understand your choices, maybe, but he always supported you. When you explained to him that you believed in what you were doing, that you felt that everyone had a right to be free and that no one had the right to dictate over anyone else, he understood that. You have to know, when he was standing on campus protesting the war, he was not against what the soldiers were doing, some of whom felt they were fighting the good fight. He was against our government's involvement in a war we shouldn't have been in, that was killing innocents on all sides. I think he was afraid for you. He knew it meant risking your life. He told me once, *I just don't want to get a telegram from the war department. Do you think they still do that?* But he was so proud, just the same." She sniffed back tears again and Steve did the same.

"Dammit, can't cry and drive. Good thing we're almost home."

"Then don't ask the tough questions when you're driving. You should know better."

Steve chuckled. "I'll invite Lou for Christmas, but you have to promise me something."

"And what would that be, sweetness?"

"Don't pull out my baby photos and show her all those pictures with me in red velvet dresses. It's undignified."

"You were so adorable. I don't know what happened." Her mother gave a sideways smirk and Steve laughed in surprise.

"What happened is I grew up and realized I look stupid in dresses. I was so happy when you started letting me wear suits on the holidays. You can show her those pictures, if you like."

"You were my little Idgie Threadgoode. You were adorable in suits too."

"Still am."

"And I'm sure Lou agrees. I saw the way she drooled over your graduation photo."

"Mother, behave."

"I will not. As long as she's drooling over my daughter, I'm all for it." As they pulled into the driveway, she said, "Oh, and ask her if she likes cranberries in her stuffing. I'm perfectly fine making it without. I know some people aren't into that sort of thing."

Steve just smiled. "Will do. See you later, Mom."

Her mother kissed her on the cheek. "Yes, you better. Now, go buy my future daughter-in-law some flowers before you see her again."

"Mother…"

"Don't take that tone with me, I know what I know."

"Good-bye, Mother."

As she was getting out of the car, she heard her mother grumble, "Raised by wolves, I swear."

Steve watched her mother walk up to her door and hollered out her window right before her mother went inside, "I love you, you pushy old bat."

Her mother turned and gave her a smile and a wave. "I love you too, you stubborn brat."

Steve laughed as she pulled out after her mother had gone into the house. She just had to shake her head. Marriage? It was way too soon to be thinking about that, but flowers were a great idea.

❖

When Lou opened the door, all she saw was a bouquet of red roses being held aloft by a hand with no owner. She giggled. "Aw, thank you, Thing." She took the flowers from the outstretched hand and sniffed them. As she did so, Steve stepped into view with a smile on her face.

"I knew you'd find a disembodied hand romantic. All the books said so." She gave Lou a meaningful kiss that almost took Lou's breath away.

Lou recovered to ask with a wry look, "Just what kind of books are you reading, anyway?"

"The Adams Family Guide to Love and Romance. It's been in the family for years." Steve reached out for Lou's arm and started hungrily kissing it. "I adore you."

Laughing, Lou said, "Je t'aime, tu dork."

Steve stopped what she was doing and looked at Lou with renewed, albeit comedic, passion, said, "Lou, that's French," and began kissing up Lou's arm again. Lou gently pulled her arm free and put both around Steve's neck. Steve responded by putting her arms around Lou's waist. "So, what did you just say to me, anyway?"

"I just said, I love you, you dork."

"Oh, that's all right then. Ready to go out?"

"Yes. I hope it's indoors. I didn't exactly dress for a picnic." Lou was dressed much as she had on their first date, in slacks and a blouse. She was a lot less nervous this time. Getting dressed hadn't been as complicated.

"It *is* indoors. Four walls, a ceiling, tables and chairs—you'll love it."

"Mm, sounds romantic."

"Nothing but the best for you, baby." Steve grinned as she put her arm around Lou's waist and led her to the car, then walked her around to the passenger side and opened the door for her.

She took Lou to an Asian restaurant on the north side of town that she had been wanting to try. It had a hibachi grill with a chef who served good food and put on an even better show. They were seated at a table with only one other couple, even though there was room for four more people. Steve was glad it wasn't full. Apparently their tablemates were too, as they sat on the far end, giving both couples as much privacy as possible.

The show was as entertaining as she'd heard. Lou was able

to catch the shrimp, the only one at the table able to do so, which made Steve smile. The chef looked at Steve and Lou and asked Steve, "First date?"

"No." She looked at Lou in question. "I think it's our third, wouldn't you say?"

Lou gave her a skeptical look. "Seems like more."

Steve laughed. "Very true."

The chef smiled big. "You two in love?"

Steve looked at Lou and they both laughed nervously. Lou grabbed Steve's hand and squeezed it. She was looking into Steve's eyes when she said, "Very much."

"Ah, good, good. I serve you first." Then the chef turned to the couple at the end of the table and said with a wink, "You're married—you should be used to waiting. Young love comes first." The couple, who were holding hands, laughed, and then the husband met Steve's gaze and lifted his glass and inclined his head. Steve lifted hers as well and returned the toast.

When the meal was prepared, the chef left them to their food. The food was as good as Steve had heard it was. As they ate, Steve looked at Lou and said, "Oh, if I don't want to be disinherited, I am to invite you to the Adams family Christmas dinner. It'll be at Mom's house. It's not required that you bring anything but yourself."

Laughing, Lou wiped her mouth with her napkin before she spoke. "The Adams family Christmas? Ooh, will we get to dump a cauldron on the carolers?"

"How could it be Christmas without that?"

"Well, count me in. So what should I bring your mother so that I can continue to make a good impression?"

"I don't think you need to worry about that. Just keep showing up—that'll impress her." Steve leaned in and gave Lou a sweet kiss, then leaned back and smiled at her.

"Well, that seems easy. I think I can manage that."

"Good. But if you're thinking presents, because there will be a gift exchange, anything book related is always a good bet.

Just not actual books. I couldn't even begin to tell you what to buy. She usually doesn't even buy books, just brings them home from work."

"Understandable. I'll think of something."

"So could you give me a clue?" Steve asked.

"I would think you'd know your mother better than I do."

She laughed. "No, I mean for you. We haven't known each other long, and I'm not sure what to get you. I want it to be right."

Lou's look softened and she caressed Steve's face. "You've already given me the best gift you could." She moved her hand down to Steve's heart and rested it there. Steve covered her hand with hers.

She broke the spell, however, by smiling and joking, "Yes, but that's not going to work every year."

Lou gently took her hand away and laughed with her. "True. I guess you're just going to have to figure that one out on your own."

"Why do I feel like this is a test?"

"Clever girl." Lou winked at her, then said with a sly grin, "Once you figure that out, you'll have to start thinking about my birthday. It'll be right around the corner, you know."

Steve stopped eating and panicked. "Oh God, I should know this, shouldn't I?"

Lou said nothing, just raised an eyebrow in expectation, then started humming the *Jeopardy* theme song.

"Crap. I think you told me this once." She started shaking her head back and forth in exasperation at her own forgetfulness. "Oh, I feel horrible. I just flunked Girlfriend One-Oh-One."

Lou laughed. "Nah, you're off the hook. I grade on a curve. I haven't told you my birthday yet."

Steve let out a sigh of relief. "Thank God."

Lou leaned in and gave Steve a quick kiss, then whispered, "It's April 4."

"Woman, you had me worried." Lou giggled. "That's plenty of time. So do you? Grade on a curve, I mean?"

Lou gave her a smile that held a very clear intention and traced a finger up Steve's thigh. "It depends on the curve."

"Why, Dr. Lou, I do believe you are learning how to flirt."

"Hmm. Sometimes we just need a good teacher." They kissed again, then rushed through their meal and hurried home.

Chapter Nineteen

L ou texted Steve: *Heard from Bill. How do you feel about going over to his and Dix's place after we leave your mother's?*

Oh God, I hope they don't want to feed us. I don't think I can take it.

LOL They did, but I said we can only do so much. We're just having wine and maybe butchering some Christmas carols.

Drunk karaoke? I'm in!

Christmas morning found Lou attempting to wrap Steve's and Lorraine's presents with shiny dark blue paper. Wrapping presents wasn't her best skill, but she put the effort in when it mattered, even though she was rarely happy with the finished product. She tried to tell herself that that didn't matter, that they wouldn't care, but it was no use. She just shook her head at her clumsy attempts to line up the paper and cut a straight line, just happy that she hadn't cut it too short. When she finished, the gifts looked passable, at least.

Steve had asked if she wanted her to pick her up on the way, but she knew that Lorraine wanted Steve to cook with her, so she had said she was happy to come over to the house on her own. Lorraine's house had lights strung around the roof and windows, which Steve had done the weekend after Thanksgiving, as well as lights in the trees and a lovely wreath on the door, replete with a red bow and pine cones. Nothing overdone. Lou smiled. It reminded her of her childhood home. The Christmas tree, with blinking lights and all the trimmings, held pride of place in the picture window. She knew Steve had helped set that up too. She and her mother had spent a day decorating and sharing memories of years past. Steve had told her it was an emotional day and she could believe it.

Now, standing on Lorraine's doorstep, she rang the bell. She could hear Christmas music playing inside. It sounded like "Jingle Bells." This time, it was Lorraine who opened the door and when she did so, she pulled a surprised Lou into a hug. Lou smiled and returned it with feeling. "Oh my God, it smells delicious in here."

Lorraine pulled her inside and closed the door behind them. "Thank you. Now come on inside, it's freezing out there. Would you like something to warm you up?"

"You mean like cocoa? Sure," Lou replied, as she set her presents under the tree, then took off her coat and put it where Lorraine instructed.

"No, dear, I meant like my loaded eggnog," she said with a wink.

Steve poked her head out of the kitchen. "She's driving, Mom. You put a full bottle of Myer's Dark in there—I saw you."

"She can handle it. I've seen her put a man twice her size flat on his back. I think she can handle a little rum." Lorraine took Lou by the arm and led her into the kitchen.

Laughing, Lou went along. She said to Steve on the way by, "She exaggerates."

"Like hell! You're a fierce warrior and it's my honor to learn from you," Lorraine said with sincerity.

Lou felt tears come to her eyes. "Thank you, Lorraine. That means a lot."

"You are welcome, dear. Now, help yourself to some 'nog, if it appeals to you, and let my prodigal child and me finish up."

Steve handed Lou a glass and kissed her on the cheek, then pretended to glare at her mother. "I did not blow all my money on prostitutes, so how can I be prodigal?"

Lorraine winked at Lou and playfully elbowed her. "Just some of the money, I guess." Lou snickered.

Steve looked horrified. "Mom, I have never spent money on prostitutes. Why do you say such things?"

"Because you are my only child and I have to pick on someone." She went up to Steve and took her chin in one hand. "Give me grandchildren, and I can have someone else to pick on." She kissed her daughter on the cheek, then turned to Lou with a questioning look, as if to say, *Well, how about some grandchildren?*

Lou thought her eyes might roll out of her head, and Lorraine threw back her head and laughed. Finally, Lou found her voice and said, "Lorraine, you're a pushy woman."

"You got that right," Steve agreed.

"Yep, I am pushy and proud. Maybe we pushy moms should start our own parade."

"No, Mom, that's a bad idea."

"You're the reason I can't have nice things."

"That's my job as your one and only child—to make your life hell." Mother and daughter exchanged grins.

Lou just sat back and enjoyed the show. She appreciated the love that was behind the banter but always close to the surface. It made her miss her own mother and the Christmases they had shared over the years, both before and after her father left. Her mother decorated traditionally, yet simply, just as Lorraine did. The smells were also the same, and those alone brought back memories of her mother preparing the turkey and all the trimmings, as well as baking pies. She'd started cooking with her mother when she was little and after a few years her mother let her be in charge of the stuffing, with her mother's recipe, of course. When she was in junior high she finally got to try baking an apple pie on her own. It was Dutch apple, she remembered, because she had always liked the crumbles on top more than the lattice crust. The memories came, and this time she couldn't stop the tears when they fell and she sniffed and wiped them away with the back of her hand.

Steve must have heard her, because she turned around, saw her wiping the tears away, and went to her. She leaned in and asked softly, "Baby, what's wrong?"

Lou wiped both eyes at once and then forced a smile. "Nothing, just reliving pleasant memories."

"Are you sure? I mean, were they all pleasant?"

Lou nodded. "Yes, I'm sure. Memories of my mom and me at Christmas. It's okay—those are good moments to remember." Lou gave Steve a peck on the lips to assure her that she was fine. She patted her on the shoulder and said, "Now go help your mother."

Steve gave her a smile and brushed a hair off Lou's forehead, then kissed her there. "Okay."

Lorraine had noticed the situation, but kindly ignored it. The only acknowledgment she made was when she came to set a dish on the table, and she gave Lou a reassuring pat on the shoulder and a warm smile.

After dinner and dessert, they gathered in the living room for presents. Steve handed Lorraine her present first, and when she unwrapped it, Lorraine held up a square piece of wood and looked at her daughter in confusion. Steve just stood there grinning. "Ah, Stephanie darling, I know they say it's the thought that counts, but I have to ask, what the hell were you thinking?"

Lou burst out laughing and looked at Steve expectantly. Steve took the wood from her mother and flipped it over and handed it back to her. "Read this."

Lorraine read aloud, "*Dear Mother, this represents the reading nook I'm going to build for you in the front window. Please don't throw this at my head.* Aw, you really are a sweet child." She stood up and hugged her and kissed her on the cheek.

"Well, you've been talking about wanting one for years. I figured it's about time you got one."

"It's never too late." She grinned at them both.

Steve looked at Lou but pointed her thumb at Lorraine. "This one never misses an opportunity."

"Nope, I take advantage of them all."

Lou placed the gift she had brought for Lorraine on Lorraine's lap and said, "Well, spoiler alert, it's not a piece of wood, but I hope you like it. You earned it."

Lorraine looked at her perplexed, then turned her attention to the present, unwrapping it gingerly. When she finally got it open, she pulled out a green sash and her eyes widened in surprise. She looked at Lou's grinning face. "Really? Already?"

"What is it, Mom?"

Instead of answering Steve, Lou said to Lorraine, "You didn't know it, but I was testing you this weekend. You passed into the next level. Congratulations."

"Oh, Mom, that's cool."

Lorraine reached over and gave Lou a hug. "Oh, thank you so much." When she pulled away she lightly swatted Lou on the shoulder. "Why didn't you tell me?"

Lou laughed. "Because I didn't want you to be nervous. You did great, by the way."

"Keep it up and you'll be a black belt in no time, just like Lou."

"Oh, I don't care if I reach that or not. I mean, it would be a great testament to the work I've put in, but I don't need that to prove anything. What's that you always say, Sifu, belts are just for holding your pants up?"

Lou laughed. "That's it. And that's a great attitude. That's why you continue to do well, because you are focusing on learning and not on achieving."

"And this is such a pretty shade of green. Perfect for the holiday." She draped the garment around her neck like a scarf for a moment, then she quickly took it off and looked at Lou with a sheepish expression. "I'm sorry, I didn't mean to be disrespectful."

Lou gave her a gentle, reassuring smile. "No, you're right, it is a lovely shade of green and it looks lovely on you. It just doesn't go with the rest of your outfit." Lorraine gave her a grateful smile in return. Lou put her hand over hers. "It's not disrespectful at all. I've often thought they would make great scarves myself—it's just not my style." Lou shifted her gaze to Steve, who was giving her such a warm look that she knew she was blushing, and she had to look away.

"Thank you, Lou. You are a great teacher."

"Thank you. Now you're going to continue your learning, yes?"

"Of course. Have to learn all I can, just in case some of those men get too fresh. A little fresh is okay."

Steve was immediately on the alert. "What men?"

Lorraine and Lou laughed together. "Would you listen to her?" Lorraine said.

"Mom...what men? Have you started dating again?"

"So what if I have? I'm old, not dead. A girl has needs."

Lou stifled a laugh.

"Oh, gross, Mom, I don't need to hear about your needs."

"Don't worry, I wasn't going to tell you."

"Thank you."

"You're welcome. Besides, I'm allowed to have a private life. I don't have to tell you everything," Lorraine replied haughtily, as she winked at Lou, who nodded in agreement.

"Fine, don't tell me. But if there's a man in your life, I'd like to meet him. After all, you're not getting any younger. It's about time I had a stepdad."

Lou couldn't hold it back anymore and laughed out loud. Lorraine appeared shocked and couldn't find the words to speak.

Steve went on in the same manner. "Don't look so surprised, Mother. Fair is fair. If you can hound me about grandchildren, I can hound you about having a father figure in my life."

"Well, I suppose you're right. Then you should know, I may have a date for New Year's Eve. I trust you kids can get along without me."

Steve said dryly, "We'll somehow make do."

Ignoring Steve, Lorraine looked at Lou and said, "Now it's my turn to give you my gift. Stephanie, can you get it for me, please?" Steve went to retrieve it and handed it to Lou with a smile.

Lou accepted the gift, which was wrapped very delicately, Lou thought, way better than she could ever hope to do. She took the paper off slowly. She opened the flat box that was big enough to hold a picture frame—which was what Lou had guessed it was, maybe holding a picture of Steve and her mother, which she would have been proud to have. But it was actually something quite different. Lou held aloft what looked like a piece of bark that had only that morning been sliced off the trunk of an oak tree, carved with a quote, and polished to perfection. It was a beautiful piece of art. Lou read aloud, "*I never teach my pupils, I only attempt to provide the conditions in which they can learn.* Einstein. I've always loved this quote. Lorraine, this is…this is beautiful. Thank you." Lou reached over and hugged her and wiped more tears from her cheeks.

"Oh, you are quite welcome. Some woman was selling her wood art at the craft show a few weeks ago and when I saw it, I just thought of you. It practically had your name on it."

Lou held it aloft, then turned it around for Steve, who stood there smiling, to see. "Oh, it sure does. It will have pride of place in my office."

"Good. Now, Stephanie, don't just stand there like a post, hand her your gift."

"I was getting to that, Mother." Steve went to the tree and picked up a smaller box and handed it to Lou as well. "I hope you like it." Then she leaned down and kissed her on the cheek.

"I'm sure I will." She opened it to reveal a book of Elsa Gidlow's poetry with a bookmark placed in the middle. Curious, she opened to the indicated page and saw that it marked a poem entitled "Love's Acolyte." She read it to herself and it brought tears to her eyes. She realized she was crying a lot that day and didn't care. She set the book aside, stood, and put her arms around Steve's neck and hugged her tight. Steve returned the embrace. Alluding to a line in the poem, she said, "Don't be ashamed. It definitely wasn't a small gift. I love it. Thank you."

"You are most welcome." Steve kissed her on the lips, wanting to linger, but knowing now was not the time or place. She just held Lou to her for as long as she could, then released her.

Lou stepped away, walked over to the tree, and retrieved her gift for Steve. She handed it to her with a small, nervous smile. "Merry Christmas, Steve."

Steve took the offering from her trepidatiously, hoping the small box didn't hold what she thought it did, and not sure how she would feel about that if it did. She almost sighed with relief when she opened the blue velvet covered box to reveal a silver necklace adorned with something she couldn't quite identify in an elongated W shape, with diamonds at five different points. She looked at Lou, confused. "It's beautiful, but I'm ashamed to say I don't know what it represents."

Lou smiled. "It's Cassiopeia. The diamonds represent star points in the constellation."

Steve gasped when she realized what it was. "Oh my God. I just…I have nothing else to say. Just…wow." Lou chuckled, but not unkindly, as Steve, at a loss for words, hugged her again.

"You're welcome." Lou knew she'd picked the right gift because Steve's eyes shone like the diamonds in the necklace.

"Let me see," Lorraine requested from the couch. Steve walked over to her mother and handed her the box, and Lorraine exclaimed appreciatively, "Oh, Lou, it's just gorgeous. I suppose it holds some special meaning for you two?"

Lou smiled at Lorraine, then at Steve. "It does."

"Steve, your girlfriend knows how to pick good gifts."

"Yes, she does."

Steve gave Lou a look of love and tenderness, but she didn't put the necklace on. Instead, she closed the box and put it in her pocket.

They all stood silently until Lorraine broke the tension and asked, "Now, who wants to help me clean the kitchen?"

Steve put her hand on Lou's arm to usher her out the door and said in a rush, "Wow, Mom, really love to stay, but we have another stop to make. Come on, Lou, don't want to keep Bill and Dix waiting."

Lou stepped out of Steve's touch with a wink over her shoulder and started to follow Lorraine into the kitchen. "They'll wait. We'll stay and help your mother. Come on, it won't kill you."

"I'm going to hold you to that." Steve dragged her feet but followed Lou and her mother out of the room.

"Stop whining." Lorraine turned to Lou and said with a shake of her head, "Raised by wolves. I tell you, that child was raised by wolves."

"You should be lucky I've learned to walk upright and I didn't lick the plate clean."

"I would have taken that as a compliment. I still would have smacked you, but I would have taken that as a compliment."

As the banter went on, Lou let it drift around her like pleasant background noise, and she couldn't stop smiling, feeling lucky to be a part of it.

❖

After they helped Lorraine clean up the kitchen, they went to Bill and Dix's as promised. They did indeed have mulled wine and sing drunken Christmas carols. They also exchanged gifts. They stayed for a few hours, then headed to Lou's house for the evening, with promises to return for the boys' New Year's Eve party the following week. When they got to Lou's house, they were still flush with the wine and in good spirits. They made slow, sensual love the rest of the evening, finally dozing off in each other's arms around two in the morning. It had been an emotional day for both of them, bringing up many memories, most of them good, but not all. Lou had found it was easier to push the bad ones away when they crept up, just by looking over at Steve as she sat next to her on Bill's couch, glass of wine in her hand, in animated conversation with Dix about her time in the service. As a history professor, Dix was interested in the human aspects of war and couldn't resist the opportunity to ask Steve questions. Bill and Lou had tried to dissuade them from talking about such topics on Christmas, but it was no use. She and Bill could only shake their heads and commiserate and have a completely different conversation without them. Being surrounded by her friends and the woman she loved made the day special for Lou.

When the Brenda Lee classic "Rockin' Around the Christmas Tree" played, Bill pulled Lou off the couch and they started to sing in animated fashion. Steve and Dix stopped talking and enjoyed the show. Realizing they had an audience, they segued into "We Wish You a Merry Christmas" then ended it with "I'll Be Home for Christmas," a song that always brought tears to Lou's eyes. It was a good thing Bill had put his arm around her shoulders at the beginning of the song, because she needed the support. That song made most of her hard memories come back, and it was tough to keep it together. When the song was over, Steve walked up to her and put her arms around her, and Lou clung to her for a moment, needing her strength. But as soon as she realized what she was doing—that she needed Steve—she gently backed away from her with a smile and whispered that she was fine. Overall, however, the whole day had been wonderful and one of the best Christmases she'd had in a long time.

Around dawn, Lou was awakened by the bedroom light coming on. She opened her eyes to see Steve frantically searching for something. She reached for her glasses on the nightstand and asked, "Baby, did you lose the necklace again?"

Distractedly, Steve replied, "Yes. And I can't find it

anywhere. I've checked all our clothes, and under the bed. It's not here. It's fucking not here." She was carelessly throwing clothes aside, clothes Lou was sure she'd already looked through.

Calmly, Lou said, "Maybe the clasp broke and it came off at your mom's or Bill's. Or in the car. We'll find it. I'll help you look." Lou got out of bed and got down on the floor as she had the last time and checked under and all around the bed, thinking it was surely nearby, that in Steve's panic she had just overlooked it. She began a methodical search around the nightstand and near the bed, trying to cover the whole area.

"I'll go check the other room." Steve walked out of the room and went into the living room to check there. They hadn't started undressing there, but if Lou was right and the clasp had broken, it could have happened anywhere. There were clothes on the couch from a day or two before where Lou had discarded them, a horrible habit Steve hated, but it was Lou's house, so she never said anything. She went through those clothes, as well as the couch, the floor around the couch, and the front door area, not finding her necklace. There was a part of her that knew Lou was probably right—it was probably in one of those other places she'd been the day before and they would find it. But what if it wasn't? What if it was gone for good? What if it had fallen off in the grocery store parking lot when her mother had sent her on a last-minute run for potatoes? What if it was right now bent and mangled after having been run over by countless other vehicles, all on last-minute shopping excursions? Or worse, someone had found it and thought it would make a great gift for someone and it was right now around someone else's neck, someone who didn't care where it had come from. Who didn't care that Steve wouldn't be able to sleep without it, someone who didn't know that it had been left for Steve in an envelope with a letter from Cairyn, telling her good-bye and that she couldn't wait for her to come home anymore. No one who found it would know or even care about any of that. It would just be some piece of jewelry to them. The perfect gift for the Capricorn in their life.

Steve suddenly felt sick and fell to her knees clutching her stomach and started to rock back and forth on the floor, arms across her chest, hands on her elbows. Her rocking intensified and her arms shifted to a crossed position over her chest, much like the sign for *I love you* she learned as a child.

She was in this position when Lou walked into the room.

Lou shook her head to indicate she was sadly not victorious from her methodical search of the bedroom. She immediately went up to Steve and knelt beside her and put her hand lightly on her shoulder. "Steve, honey, it'll be okay, we'll find it. We just have to keep looking. We found it last time, and we'll find it again."

Steve didn't stop her rocking. If anything, its frequency increased and she didn't respond.

"Honey? Come on, let's keep looking." Lou moved her hand to the back of Steve's arm, to help her off the floor.

Steve cried out in a panicked voice, "Don't touch me!" and swung her left hand back in a warding off gesture. Her hand made contact with Lou's face, hitting her nose and glasses, breaking the glasses at the nosepiece, but thankfully not Lou's nose.

The impact was painful and surprising, and Lou rocked back on her heels, her glasses falling off her face, clutching her nose, which had started to bleed. Steve was still rocking and was oblivious to her. When Lou saw the blood on her fingers, memories of her father came rushing back of the first time he had hit her and how much her nose had bled. Just like the first time, she grabbed a T-shirt off the floor and held it to her nose to stop the bleeding. Her voice was muffled around the shirt when she said to Steve, "Get out."

Steve started to come around, about ten minutes after the initial onset of her panic attack. She took a few breaths and swallowed and put her head down. Softly she said, "I have to find it."

A little louder and more clearly, Lou said, "I said, get out. Get out of my house. You're not doing that to me again. Just go!"

Startled, Steve turned around and looked at Lou as if for the first time. Her eyes widened when she saw the blood and took in the broken glasses on the floor. Confusion was written all over her face when she asked, "What happened?"

"Just go."

Steve reached out to her, but Lou backed away and stood up, then walked toward her bathroom. Steve stood up slowly, still feeling shaky. She called out, "Lou, if I did that, I'm sorry."

From behind the bathroom door, Lou said, "Go, just get the fuck out, goddammit."

"Lou…?" But Lou said nothing more. Steve heard running water and knew that Lou was done talking to her. She leaned her head against the door and cried. "I'm sorry. I'm so sorry. I love you." It was the only thing she could think to say. She stood there for a few more minutes, her head on the door and her eyes closed, tears on her cheeks. But the door never opened, and after a while she went back to Lou's room and got dressed, took one last look at the bed, the bed where they had declared their love for each other just a few hours before, and left the room, taking one last look at the impenetrableness of the closed bathroom door. She whispered again, "I love you, Lou." Then she walked out of the house, wishing she hadn't left her car at her mother's the night before when she and Lou had gone to Bill and Dix's.

As she walked down the street, putting some distance between herself and Lou's house, she pulled out her phone and called a cab, not wanting to wake her mother up so early, but also not wanting to have to explain.

CHAPTER TWENTY

Lou had heard Steve's first declaration of love. When the bleeding stopped, she had thrown the bloody T-shirt on the counter and began to splash her face, grateful her nose hadn't broken a second time. Instead of reviewing the situation that had just played out, her mind went to practical things, such as wondering when and where she would be able to get a new pair of glasses over the holiday and whether or not she still had her previous pair that, though a slightly different prescription, would suffice in the meantime. She shut out thoughts of her father and thoughts of the woman who'd just left her house, possibly for the last time. She concentrated on cleaning her face and decided to go ahead and take a shower, since she was in there.

Now, two days later, Lou was sitting alone in her favorite café, laptop open, working on her novel. She was making good progress and felt good with how the story was going. She was always happy when she was able to just focus on her writing. She found it very relaxing. She was on her second cup of coffee and planned to spend the rest of her Christmas holiday doing what she was doing now: writing and drinking coffee. Her classes for the following semester were mostly already planned out because she was teaching the same classes as she had the previous spring, with only one new prep, which meant she only needed to take a day to tweak the other syllabuses for those other classes. The one for the new class she had worked on the previous month during a rare moment when she had gotten ahead on her grading. Her research project, the one she had been working on all semester, the one she was going to submit to a conference next summer, was also in a good place. The research and writing were done— she just had to edit it, make sure it adhered to the conference committee's guidelines, and get it turned in on time. So it was a relief to be doing something just for herself, which is what writing her novel was.

She hadn't spoken to Steve since she'd told her to leave, and she had ignored her calls and texts, deleted her voice mails. She wasn't ready to listen to them and she sure as hell wasn't ready to forgive her. Luckily, she had been able to get her glasses repaired yesterday and only had to wear the old pair for a day, so her eyes weren't really bothered by the temporary change. She did miss Steve and wished it hadn't happened, but she wasn't ready to let her back in her life yet. It just seemed too risky. How could she trust that it wouldn't happen again?

Sure, the slap was an accident, an involuntary reaction while Steve was in the midst of a panic attack, the first time Lou had ever seen her have one. But if that was something that was going to happen more often, Lou knew she didn't want to be around it. It was unhealthy. But knowing that didn't stop her heart from breaking at the thought that something that started so beautifully could end so abruptly and harshly. She knew she should have avoided Steve when she found out she was ex-military, just listened to her instincts and not flirted with her when Lorraine had introduced them, not flirted with her later when she called. *Last time I date a soldier.* They were too unpredictable.

Just then, she heard a pleasant-sounding voice say, "Hello again."

She looked up to see the ROTC officer who had asked her out the last time they had run into each other. She groaned inwardly, but tried not to show her annoyance at being interrupted. "Hello, Cadet Bolen, how are you?"

Bolen appeared surprised by how Lou addressed her and

didn't seem sure how to react. She replied, "I'm doing well, Dr. Silver. Having a good break so far?"

Instead of replying to the question put to her, Lou asked one of her own instead. "I meant to ask you last time we saw each other, how do you know my name, anyway? I know you're not one of my students, and I've never introduced myself to you."

Bolen sat down in the chair opposite Lou at the table, even though she hadn't been invited, and stretched her long legs out into the aisle. She wouldn't be in anyone's way, as they were at the back of the café and no one would need to come back that way. She looked at Lou a little sheepishly and blushed. "Oh, uh, I asked."

Lou noted the blush but ignored it. Instead, she narrowed her eyes at Bolen and asked, "Asked who? Why?"

"I asked Tabitha, the barista. She knows everybody."

"And my other question?"

Bolen squirmed uncomfortably in her chair. "Are you like this in the classroom?" She tried to smile but it faltered when Lou was unmoved.

"Like what?"

"Nothing. Nothing bad, I mean. Just determined to get answers, I guess."

"Only when someone's not answering my questions. It's a fair question."

"True." Bolen let out a defeated sigh. "Okay. I asked because I like you. I wanted to know who you were so that I could ask you out. I still like you, by the way, but I respect your answer and your relationship."

This time Lou rewarded her with a small smile. "I appreciate that." Lou saved her document and closed the laptop, admitting defeat and squelching any hope that she was going to get more writing done. "Tell me something, Bolen…"

"Mel."

"Okay. Tell me something, Mel, do you plan to make the Army a career after your initial service agreement is over?" She knew the ROTC scholarship students had to agree to a term of service of eight years, which they could fulfill in a variety of ways. She had considered it herself while in high school when her father was in Iraq. She'd thought it would be the best way she could honor him and serve her country, the country that he had taught her to take pride in, but when he had come home mentally broken, she had decided against it. She had been upset with the Army and more than a little upset with her country for allowing her father's injury to happen.

"No. I honestly don't want to. I mean, I did in the beginning, and it was a great way to help my parents pay for college, but since the election, I just can't. How can I fight the wars of a government I don't trust, who are just playing playground games of one-upmanship, instead of helping people who are actually in need? I know it's not necessarily a new thing, but I think it's worse now than it's ever been. I'm not going to put my life on the line for that. I'm only a freshman, so I have the rest of the year to decide if I want to quit or not. I have until the first day of my sophomore year to quit, or I have to reimburse the scholarship money."

Lou nearly spat out her coffee. Bolen was younger than she thought. Instead of commenting on that, however, she went a different way. "So what will you do if you leave the ROTC?"

"You mean to pay for college, or after college?"

Lou shrugged. "Both, I guess. What's your major?"

"I honestly haven't decided yet. I'm leaning toward computers, but that's because that's what my father suggested I do. It's what he does and there's always money there."

"Yes and no. But that's not really the point. What do you want to do?" Advising was part of Lou's job, and she enjoyed it, but it was usually her own students she met with for advising, not undeclareds.

"Hmm, I don't know." Bolen looked perplexed for a moment and gave Lou a blank look.

"Well, in my own department—that is, if you have an interest in theater by chance—there's always lighting design. Put those computer skills, along with so many other things, to use in a practical, yet fun way."

Bolen looked interested, then laughed and shook her head. "I don't think that's exactly what my father had in mind."

"Whose future is it, yours or his?" Before Mel could answer, Lou went on. "This is your time now, Mel. And if you can get a scholarship some other way, you won't feel as guilty about majoring in whatever you want. Which you shouldn't anyway."

Mel nodded thoughtfully. "I know you're right. It's just hard to break out of that mold, you know? Don't want to disappoint your parents."

"Trust me, there are bigger decisions you will make in life that have far more chance of disappointing your parents than what you major in in college." Bolen laughed. "But if they're supportive of you, then they'll get over it, especially once they see how happy you are in whatever it is you settle on. Just remember, you have some time to decide."

"Yeah, but not much. You know, it's just occurred to me that you haven't pushed your major. I mean, what you teach. Is that because you don't think it'd be right for me?"

"Not at all! I think you would do well in stage combat. I just didn't want to presume…"

"That because I was willing to play soldier for a while, that I like fighting?" Mel asked dubiously.

"Precisely. Stage combat isn't for everyone, of course. And unlike being a soldier, it's not real. Injuries can sometimes occur, but they are rarely fatal." She gave Mel a weak smile.

Mel chuckled. "Okay. Something to chew on." She looked thoughtful for a moment, then said, "Well, this whole conversation took a turn. Talking about my future plans wasn't exactly what I had in mind when I sat down." She gave Lou a flirtatious smile, but it was obvious that this time she was only teasing.

Instead of rising to the bait, Lou brushed the smile aside and narrowed her eyes at the younger woman. "Oh, please. Let's move past that, shall we?"

"I was only teasing, Lou."

"As an undergrad, I really wish you'd address me as Dr. Silver. Maybe when you're a grad student you can call me by my first name. But only if you're *my* student. Until then, I didn't spend all this money for you to talk to me as if we grew up together." Though her words were stern, her voice was kind, and after a moment or two, she smiled across the table at Mel.

Mel laughed. "Understood, Dr. Silver." Mel stood and pushed her chair in. "Thank you for the real talk. You have definitely given me a lot to think about. Question—if I became a stage combat major, would you be my advisor?"

"Maybe. I don't assign that, but you could request me. There are forms…" Lou trailed off.

Now Mel grinned. "Okay. I'll think about it. You might be seeing me again, but in your office next time."

"I look forward to it." Bolen took her leave and Lou decided to pack up for the day and do the same. Her thoughts about Steve were no more clear in her head than they had been before.

Chapter Twenty-one

Steve was in her garage, hitting the heavy bag with such force and steady concentration that she didn't hear her mother's car pull up in the driveway, or hear her call her name, until there she was, standing in the doorway that led from the garage into the kitchen. She just continued to hit the bag with force and determination. She didn't pause in what she was doing until she saw the lights flicker in the garage and finally turned to her mother. She took off her gloves and hung them up. "Hey." She was out of breath and sweaty from the brief but intense workout. She took a drink from the water bottle she had on the bench, trying to avoid her mother for as long as possible.

Her mother eyed her shrewdly, however, and asked, "Are you all right?"

Catching her breath, Steve said, "I'm fine. What are you doing here?"

"I just wanted to see you. I've tried calling but you haven't answered my calls. I was hoping you weren't sick. Hoping maybe you and Lou were just cuddled up somewhere, since I know she has time off right now. And when she didn't answer my calls either, I thought that must be it. But her car's not here, so…" Lorraine trailed off, perhaps seeing the pain Steve knew must be visible in her eyes and realizing she'd struck a nerve. "Is everything all right with you two?"

"I need a shower." Steve started to walk past her mother without answering her last question.

"Stephanie Marie Adams," her mother called after her, "don't walk away from me. I want you to answer my question."

Steve sighed and stopped in her tracks. "Mother, not now. Can we do this another time?"

"Do what? I didn't come over here for a simple dinner date with my daughter. I came over here because something doesn't feel right, and I want to get to the bottom of it. Tell me I'm wrong, convince me of it, and I'll go away." Her mother crossed her arms over her chest and blocked the door to the kitchen so that Steve's only choice would be to go out through the garage door if she wanted to escape that badly.

"Fine, you want to know what's going on? I screwed up and she kicked me out. And don't worry, she's not answering my calls either."

"What do you mean you screwed up? Last I saw, you were having a great holiday. What happened after you left my house?"

"I don't want to go into this, Mom. I just want to put it behind me."

"Stephanie…" There was a note of warning in her voice that was hard to ignore. Steve had never been able to resist it. She caved every time.

"I was having a panic attack. She came up behind me and put her hand on my neck. I didn't realize how close she was—I just knew I didn't want to be touched. I swung my arm back and hit her in the face. Broke her glasses and bloodied her nose. She kicked me out and hasn't spoken to me since. Now I need to shower." Her mother stepped aside, stunned, and Steve walked into the house, heading toward her bathroom.

Her mother followed. "And that's why she hasn't spoken to you? But it was an accident. I'm sure she must see that."

"There's more to it than that."

Her mother eyed her with a new suspicion. "Has it happened before?"

"No! Jeez, Mom. I don't hit women. It really was just an accident. I just meant...never mind, I don't know if she'd want me sharing too much from her past. The point is, I know that what happened probably brought up bad memories for her, and she's probably seeing the situation more through that than what actually happened. She's got baggage, Mom, and I'm paying the price for it."

"Well, so do you. She knows about Cairyn now, I take it?"

"Yeah. I told her everything."

"And she was willing to stand by you and love you and make room for Cairyn, knowing she would always be a part of you?"

"Yeah."

"Then whatever her baggage is, if it's something she needs to let go of, and if you love her, you need to see what you can do about helping her do that."

"How am I supposed to do that if she won't talk to me?"

"You're the romantic one, figure it out."

"I don't think a romantic gesture is going to get me out of this. This is much deeper than that. This goes back to childhood."

"I suspected as much. Just let her know you love her and will stand by her and help her unpack all that baggage."

"I don't think it's going to be that simple. Would be nice, though."

Her mother put her hands on her shoulders. "Darling, sometimes you have to fight for the things that matter, instead of standing on the sidelines and letting them happen. Isn't that why you joined the Army in the first place?" Steve started to speak but her mom cut her off. "And don't tell me it's not the same thing, because it is. The only thing better than love of country is love of family, and she's family. Don't you give up on her." Her mother kissed her on the cheek, and Steve held tightly to her.

It only took a moment for Steve's tears to flow and for the sound of her sniffles to echo in the room.

"You just cry it out, baby, just cry it out." Her mother began to slowly sway back and forth as Steve cried the first time since Cairyn's death.

❖

Later that night after her mother left, Steve was having a restless sleep. She still hadn't found her necklace, and it had always served as a talisman to ward off any bad dreams. Without it, sleep didn't come easily and she hadn't had a restful night since Christmas. Tonight was no exception. Her dreams shifted from when she'd heard the news that Cairyn had taken her life, to the time before when she had tried but had been found by Lorraine. Steve hadn't been able to make it home for that and she had always regretted it. She had called Cairyn as much as she could, which wasn't that often, but there wasn't anything she could do about that. When she would call, Cairyn didn't say much, other than that she missed her. And she'd cried a lot. Steve would cry with her and apologize for being gone. It was all she could do, really. For the first time since she had joined the Army, she'd wanted to walk away from it. She wanted to leave the battles for someone else to fight, since she had one more important at home. But she had signed her name and her life over to the US government, and she had to see it through.

This night, she dreamed of the hospital where Cairyn stayed after her first attempt. She saw her in her bed, in her hospital gown, sitting up, her lustrous brown hair a mess, a bemused smile on her face. Steve didn't know why her brain was showing her this—she had never seen Cairyn in the hospital. She didn't even think it had been described to her. But she was curious what was going to happen, so when Cairyn held up her hand to her and beckoned her over, she went and took Cairyn's hand in hers, then leaned down and kissed her on the cheek. When she got close to Cairyn, she immediately smelled a faint hint of coconut and vanilla, the soap she preferred, and Steve breathed it in, holding on to it for as long as she could.

After a moment, she stood up and smiled at her fiancée. "I'm sorry I couldn't come before."

Cairyn gave her a forgiving smile. "It's okay. You had a job to do. I just, I couldn't…"

Steve squeezed her hand. "I know, honey, I know. It's okay."

"Do you? Do you understand?"

"I think I do. You needed me at home and I let you down. I promised to always be there for you and I let you down." Steve looked away. She had too much guilt to look Cairyn in the eyes.

"Oh God, no, baby, no, that's not it." Cairyn grasped Steve's hand firmly in hers and tried to get Steve to look at her. "You were always there for me."

"You're just saying that to make me feel better, but if I was always there for you, why did you do what you did? Why couldn't you handle being alone? Whatever it was doesn't matter, though—I said I would take care of you, and I didn't, and this is my fault."

"My God, do you have to take credit for my death?" Now Cairyn sounded frustrated and released Steve's hand. "Can't I have one thing that's mine? Steve, I did this…me. This was a choice I made because I just couldn't handle things anymore. I know it sounded like I was blaming you, but I wasn't. Steve, I'm sorry I put that guilt on you. That wasn't right." Now her look softened and she reached for Steve's hand again.

"But some of the blame is mine, though."

"No, it's not. You didn't give me my demons, others did. I had been fighting them all my life. When I met you, I thought I had things under control, and you…I thought you were my knight in shining armor. You were so brave and strong, and I thought you would be my anchor, so I clung to you. Then when you shipped out, I was adrift."

Tears choked Steve's voice when she said, "I know."

"Listen. I was adrift because I had never learned how to anchor myself. I had no right to put that on you. I am so sorry, honey. I really hope you can forgive me."

The tears were now dripping off Steve's face onto her shirt and she wiped them away. "There's nothing to forgive."

"Yes, there is. I know what's been happening to you. I know about the nightmares and the panic attacks. I know how you ran away from the Army. You have to stop running, Steve."

"I didn't go AWOL. I served my time is all. I left the proper way."

"Doesn't mean anything, and that's not my point."

"I needed to grieve. And with the panic attacks, I wasn't fit anymore."

"They would have let you do therapy, if you'd worked with them. But you didn't tell them, did you? You did your time, then got out as soon as you could."

"I got help, Cairyn. They're much better than they were."

"Yes, they are. But they are still holding you back, keeping you from moving on. You lost my necklace for a reason, Steve. Don't you realize that?" There was such love in Cairyn's deep brown eyes, and they glistened with unshed tears.

"You know about that?"

Cairyn chuckled softly. "Oh, honey, this is a dream. I'm just a part of you—you know that. And I know everything. I can see your heart. I know you're grieving right now, but it's not for me. You don't need that necklace to hold on to me. You know I'm always here, whenever you close your eyes. But she's a part of you too now. It was time to let go of the necklace, but don't let go of her."

Steve let out a strangled cry. "But how can I do that when she won't talk to me?"

Cairyn laughed again. "Steve, I'm dead, what are you asking me for?" Steve let out a surprised laugh. "You know where she lives, you know where she works, you know where she's going to be New Year's Eve. You've always been romantic—figure something out."

"You and my mother, I swear, you both think I'm some romantic hero or something. But there are worse things, I guess."

"Who was it who got one of her security guard buddies to let us up on the roof of the tallest building in Oklahoma City one Fourth of July so we could watch fireworks? Huh?" Cairyn grinned and merriment danced in her eyes as she teased Steve.

"I suppose so."

"You suppose so." Cairyn shook her head in exaggeration, then said softly, "Steve, come here."

Steve stepped closer and sat down in the chair that was next to the bed so that she could lean in. "I'm here."

"Let me go, Steve. It's time."

"I can't."

"Yes, you can. It's okay—I've got this. It's okay."

"No." Steve whimpered, then put her head on the side of the bed, clutching Cairyn's hand.

Cairyn delicately disengaged her hand and ran it through Steve's hair. "It's okay, baby, it's okay. It's okay…"

Steve woke up with a start, her face wet with tears. Instinctively, she reached over to the nightstand for the Capricorn pendant, but her hands came up empty. Instead, they found a small box, the box from Lou that held the necklace she had given her at Christmas. She sat up and reached for the box, then turned her bedside light on, automatically blinking at the sudden glare. She opened the box and looked at the five diamonds that represented the five star points in Cassiopeia and ran her finger over them delicately and started to smile. She gingerly took the necklace out of its box and put it around her neck, shivering at the coldness of the metal as it touched her neck. Then she put the box back on her nightstand. She put her hand over the constellation and sighed, then lay back down and closed her eyes.

Chapter Twenty-two

L ou left the campus gym, where she had gone for her workout. With most of the students gone for the winter break, the place was practically deserted, with only a couple of students scattered about, dedicated lifters from the looks of them. She had enjoyed a nice, quiet workout without running into anyone she knew and had no embarrassing encounters, for which she was grateful. On the drive home, her phone buzzed to indicate she had a text message. She read it when she came to a stoplight. She was relieved it was from Bill, making sure she was coming to the New Year's Eve party. She didn't have a chance to text back before the light changed, but she was only a few minutes from home and it wasn't urgent, so she waited to answer until she was in her driveway.

Yes, I'll be there, but I'm flying solo.

Since when?

I'll tell you later.

She was on her doorstep when the phone gave off its continual buzz and she looked down to see he was calling her. She should have known he wouldn't be put off that easily. She considered not answering it, but figured talking to him shouldn't be too painful. She answered the phone with one hand while she unlocked her front door with the other, thankful she had left her workout clothes in the car so that she had less to juggle. "Hello, Bill."

"Don't *Hello, Bill* me, what do you mean you're not bringing Steve to the party? What have I missed?"

As Lou closed her front door, she said, "I don't want to go into it, just that we're done." There was a note of finality in her voice that was hard to argue with and most people didn't when they heard her take that tone.

"Since when?" Bill wasn't most people. "Last time I saw you, you were slobbering all over each other. You practically made a lesbian baby on my couch when you thought no one was looking. How can you be done?"

Despite her mood, she couldn't help smiling at the image he created. "I kissed her one time on the couch. You make it sound like we were making out."

"There was tongue. I know tongue when I see it."

Lou chuckled. "There was no tongue. And there wasn't then, nor will there ever be any lesbian babies with her. Sorry to disappoint you." She immediately thought of Lorraine and her chiding Steve for grandchildren and felt a pang at losing her relationship with the woman. She knew that she would have to recommend a different instructor for her.

"What the hell happened?"

Lou sighed. "Suffice it to say, I don't appreciate being hit. That's kind of a deal breaker for me." She threw her keys on the kitchen table, then reached in the fridge for a fresh bottle of water. After opening it and taking a refreshing sip, she sat down at the table.

"That bitch hit you? Did you file charges?"

"Simmer down, it wasn't that bad."

"It was bad enough to break up with her, and don't downplay it."

"Sorry, maybe I up-played it. It was an accident." Bill scoffed, but before he could speak, she cut him off. "It was. It's not like I said I ran into a door. I just meant that the circumstances around it were accidental, but considering how it happened, it

could happen again. And I don't want to be around if it does."
She shrugged as if he could see her through the phone.

"Could you be more vague?"

"I could, but I choose not to."

"I'm sorry, honey." Bill softened his voice. "I'm just worried about you. If it truly was an accident, then why'd you break up with her?"

Lou took a moment before she responded. When she finally did, she said, "It just put me in a bad place. A place I don't like to be. A place I told myself I would never be again. I can't go back to that."

"Oh, honey…"

"Listen, Bill, I should go. It is okay if I just bring me, right?"

"Of course, sweetie. You are more than enough."

Warmed by his words, Lou smiled.

Bill *tsk*ed. "Too bad about Sgt. Hottie, though. I really thought she had potential."

"Why do you always give the women I date very descriptive nicknames? You called my last girlfriend All the Way May, which wasn't even her name. I didn't understand it then, and I don't understand it now."

"I do it because it's fun."

"Fun for you, maybe."

"Yes, and? By the way, I called her that because she loved sports and she looked a little too much *A League of Their Own* for my taste."

"Well, you weren't the one dating her."

"Thank the goddess."

Lou scoffed. "Anyway, I'll see you at the party."

Bill said in a more serious tone, "Honey, I'm here if you want to have a real conversation about this. Whatever really happened, I'm always on your side."

"I know. I appreciate it and I thank you. I'll talk to you later."
She ended the call and put the phone on the table, stretching her

legs out in front of her, holding the bottle of water on her stomach, staring into space. She leaned forward, set the bottle on the table, then laid her head on her arms and let out a big sigh. "Adulting is too fucking hard."

❖

Later that night, Lou had trouble sleeping. It'd been weeks since she had dreamed about her father, but this dream wasn't like the last time. Instead of dreaming about the first time he had hit her and the last time she ever kissed Tanya, this time she dreamed about something more pleasant. It was reminiscent of all those times as a child when they would lie out in the backyard on the grass, looking up at the stars, him teaching her the constellations. But it was different this time. This time, she was herself, at her present age, and he was the age he had been when she last saw him. But instead of looking at her in wonderment, at the fact that his child had just broken his wrist, or in distaste, as he had when he caught her kissing Tanya several months earlier, when she came upon him in this dream, he looked up and smiled.

"Well hello, girlie, 'bout time you showed up. What took you so long?"

"Sorry I'm late." It was all she could think to say, though she wasn't sure why she was apologizing, other than habit. She lay down beside him on the grass and put her arms behind her head.

"It's all right. Not much out tonight, too much cloud cover."

"That's okay, we still know they're there. They're always there," Lou replied wistfully.

"That's right. We can always count on that."

"I've always thought it was sad, though, that the stars we see are actually long dead by the time we see them."

Her father looked at her sharply. "Who told you that?"

"You did, didn't you?"

"That wasn't me. Don't believe everything you see on that damn internet bullshit." Lou snickered. Her father pointed up to the sky. "Those are just as alive as you and me." He turned to her sheepishly, then said, "Well, as you." Lou smiled and he went on. "They're just really old. They live for a very long time. There are stars in Andromeda that are over two million years old."

"Wow," Lou whispered.

"That's right. We got nothing on them. It almost doesn't seem fair, does it? Why do we only get these really short lives that only last a nanosecond in the grand scheme of things, and those little twinkling bastards get to go on, doing their thing for millennia? I don't know, but I tell ya, if there's a creator, I'm going to ask him that question. I didn't get nearly enough time with you and your mother as I wanted. But that wasn't all his fault."

"Dad…"

"It's true and I know it. I had choices and I made all the wrong ones. I let you and your mother down. Mostly you." He sat up and turned to face Lou, who mimicked his posture. "I'm sorry, Louise. I wasn't the father you deserved. I was a rotten son of a bitch a good lot of the time, and to say you deserved better is the biggest understatement of all time. I'm so sorry, Louie."

Her father was the only one who ever called her that. Her mother hated it. Her mother hadn't even liked the diminutive Lou, but Lou had insisted and she had caved on it, though still called her Louise more often than not. But something about this conversation didn't sit well with her and she just shook her head in denial. "See, that's how I know this is a dream. My father would never apologize to me. He was never sorry for anything he did. I need to figure out how to wake myself up from this and get out of here." Lou moved to stand up, but her father reached out and clamped down on her arm. With vehemence, she snarled, "Let go of me, old man, and stay out of my dreams!" She shook him off and stood up and started to walk away, but he called her name and his voice stopped her quicker than his grip ever could.

"Are you ever going to let go of your anger and stop hating me?"

She turned on her heel, stalked back up to him, and pointed a finger in his face. "I did let it go, but you won't leave me alone. You're *dead*, get it? You're dead. So act like it. Leave me alone!"

"You haven't gotten over your anger—you just keep pushing it aside. You think you've buried it, but it's not even buried that deep. It's right there, right now, and you want to hit me, but you also don't want to be like me, so you bury those feelings and you run away. You gotta stop running, girlie, and look at what you're leaving behind."

"I'm trying to leave you behind, but you won't go away."

"I'm not talking about me. She didn't mean it, baby. Don't make her pay for my mistakes."

"I'm not talking about this with you."

"Fine. But just put the blame where it belongs."

"She hit me—don't you get that? Accident or not, she fucking hit me, and who's to say it won't happen again? And don't you dare say *love*, because love is not the answer to everything, and it does not conquer all. That's a bullshit lie women have been fed, and many stay in bad relationships because they bought into it. Or some asshole told them that's what happens. I'm not falling for it. Some people don't get a happily ever after. Sometimes things just end, period."

"And often too soon."

Lou's eyes opened and she was back in her darkened bedroom, clutching a pillow to her chest, the covers thrown off. She threw the pillow aside and sat up, then reached for her glasses, not bothering to turn on the light. She got out of bad and padded through her house to the door that led to the small backyard and stood there in her boxers and Army T-shirt in the moonlight and looked up at the stars. Sirius was shining bright tonight. She automatically thought of Homer and began to recite to herself, "*Beneath the rage of burning Sirius rise...*" She hugged her arms to herself and shivered, then closed the door and shuffled back to her room, but not to sleep. Instead, she turned on the light and took the book of poetry Steve had given her for Christmas off the corner of her nightstand and settled back into bed with it, pulling the covers up to her waist. Gidlow was always more pleasant than Homer any day of the week.

CHAPTER TWENTY-THREE

On Saturday, Lou waited for Lorraine on the mat at the Wushuguan. She was dressed to teach, but she wasn't sure if she was going to. She had talked to one of the other instructors there and he had agreed to add Lorraine to his schedule, as he was the only one who had time on the weekends when Lorraine normally saw Lou. Lou paced with her hands on her hips, waiting for Lorraine to arrive.

When Lorraine finally walked in, she stopped midstride when they made eye contact. Lorraine looked just as nervous as Lou felt, but she took a deep breath and stepped forward to face her. "Hello, Lou."

Lou replied with a weak smile, "Hello, Lorraine. We need to talk."

"You're not breaking up with me too, are you?" Lorraine gave her a forced jovial smile and Lou chuckled.

But she sobered when she said, "I think it's for the best, don't you?"

"No, I do not. I don't see why what's happening between you and my daughter should affect us. I'm here to learn kung fu from you, not anyone else in this joint. I want the best." Lorraine crossed her arms over her chest and stood in front of Lou defiantly.

"I appreciate that."

"So are we going to do this, or what?" Without waiting for a reply, Lorraine strode onto the mat and waited for Lou to join her and start the lesson.

Amused, Lou said, "I guess we are." The rest of the session went well and they both focused on the task at hand. Lou realized that maybe she could teach Lorraine and have it just be about that. Steve needn't be a part of their relationship. She was glad. She would miss Lorraine if she had to stop teaching her. When she had come to the decision to find another instructor for her, it had been painful.

Once the session was over, they were both toweling the sweat off and getting drinks of water on the sidelines. Lorraine said, "I totally understand, you know? I would have broken up with her too, if I were you."

Lou checked herself from giving Lorraine a harsh look and, instead, did her best to tamp down her emotions. "Thank you. I'd really rather not talk about it, if that's okay."

"No, perfectly understandable. I wasn't going to get into your business. I just want you to know, I don't approve of that sort of thing at all, and I gave her a major dressing down for it. She knows better than to hit a woman. Her father and I taught her respect for women and this was uncalled for. So I understand. I told her she was lucky someone as wonderful as you went out with her in the first place."

"Now wait, I don't know what she told you happened, but I think you got the wrong impression. It wasn't a domestic violence type of situation. It was an accident. She was having a panic attack at the time. I'm not trying to excuse it, but she wasn't really hitting me. She just put her arm up like this"—Lou put her arm up to demonstrate—"but I was in the wrong place at the wrong time." She closed her eyes and hung her head. When she opened her eyes again, she saw Lorraine looking at her with a kind smile. "I overreacted, didn't I?"

Lorraine put her hands on Lou's shoulders. "No, honey, you acted fine. That's what you needed to do in that moment. That's just the place that situation put you in. You were following your instincts."

"But my instincts were wrong."

"Your instincts are there to protect you. Now, I don't know what's in your past—Steve's kept your secrets, just as she's kept Cairyn's—but I do know that whatever it is, you're not going to get past it by running away from it."

"Steve told you that I—"

"No, as I said, she hasn't told me anything, she never would. But we all have a past. Things we don't want to think about anymore but sometimes can't help it. When I met Steve's father…when I met that lovely man, I hated men. I never wanted one to touch me again. Now, I won't go into all that, but suffice it to say, if I hadn't gotten help from the campus counseling office, I wouldn't have been ready to let Steven into my life when he showed up. Don't misunderstand me—it took a while before I could trust again, and it wasn't like I met the man of my dreams and everything was right with the world. Oh no, there was a healing process. And even after we started dating, I made him take things real slow. And he was so patient. He didn't mind waiting for me, he said." Lorraine smiled at the memories. She caressed Lou's cheek. "I'm not telling you to let bygones be bygones. I'm telling you to put one foot in front of the other and see where the path leads."

Lou wiped a tear from her eye and nodded. "Thank you, Lorraine. I needed that."

"I know, sugar. Here, you take this. When the time is right, you call this number and you tell them what you need. They'll be glad to help."

Lou looked at the card Lorraine put in her hand. "What is this?"

"That's the doctor Steve used for her panic attacks. Trust me when I say they have gotten better, though she's still on her journey. We all have to walk one, sometimes alone. Sometimes alone is best. For a while."

"You are a wise woman, Lorraine."

Lorraine let go of Lou and backed up and wiped her eyes. She chuckled at Lou's words. "I've been called a lot of things, but I don't think I've been called wise before."

"Well, you are. Thank you. I'll give them a call."

"Good."

Lou took a deep breath, putting steel in her spine, and gave Lorraine a genuine smile, then looked at the older woman shrewdly. "Did you really give her a piece of your mind?"

Lorraine laughed. "Oh, honey, at my age, I don't have any to spare."

Lou surprised herself by laughing and it felt good. They walked out together in good spirits and Lorraine hugged her at her car. For the first time in years, Lou felt like she was part of a family. She looked up to the bright sky overhead and whispered, "I love you, Mom. I miss you." Then she got in her Jeep and drove home. Before she went into the house, she pulled out her gym bag and all the empty coffee cups from the back seat. Once she got inside, she dumped the coffee cups into the trash and put her clothes into the wash. Feeling better than she'd felt in days, she pulled out her phone and opened up her music app and looked for a good song to play, finally settling on an Elvis song. She smiled when she realized what it was. "Yeah, I'm all shook up too, Elvis." She let Elvis work his magic on her, and she got lost in the music, this time, not trying to summon the muse, just to soothe her soul.

Chapter Twenty-four

The next day, Lou dressed in black slacks, a long-sleeved white blouse, and a black bow tie that had diamonds on the tips. She smiled when she looked at herself in the mirror. She often didn't do the butch look at all, but she was feeling festive tonight. Even though she and Steve weren't back together, she felt it would happen in its own time, when it was right. She really did love her. She was ready to make some positive steps in her life, and she wanted them to include Steve. She wasn't quite ready for them to ride off into the sunset together yet, but all things in time. As Lorraine pointed out, sometimes you have to take your journey alone for a while, but eventually, when the time was right, you could let the right one join you on the path.

Taking one last look in the mirror, she exhaled and blew a stray hair off her face at the same time. "You got this." Then she was out the door.

Dix greeted her knock and kissed her on the cheek. Bill came up to her shortly after she got there and hugged her. When he pulled back, he said, "I'm glad you're here. There's someone I want you to meet."

"Bill, please tell me you're not going to set me up with someone."

"Would I do that to you?"

"What was that woman's name you introduced me to at last year's party?"

"I don't know what you're talking about."

"Uh-huh. She was old enough to be my grandmother, Bill."

"You exaggerate. Walk this way."

"Oh, I'll walk this way, but I'll run if it looks like you're doing the same thing again." Bill steered her to a couple on the other side of the living room, one a tall, gorgeous redhead with long curly hair who looked about Bolen's age if she was a day, and her much shorter partner, with dark brown hair pulled into a braid, who stood with one arm around her waist. The woman with the braid was easily her age, her partner much younger, and Lou suddenly knew who she was standing with and smiled when both women turned to greet her at Bill's introduction.

"Rory, Maggie, I want you to meet Lou, your replacement."

Maggie stuck out her hand and smiled. "Nice to meet you. Bill mentioned that he has replaced me. So fickle, that one." She grinned up at Bill, who tried to look shocked.

"I have not replaced you, love, but I have to have my daily dose of lesbian vibes, otherwise I'll be deficient."

Lou playfully narrowed her eyes at him. "That's not what makes you deficient."

They all laughed as Bill put his hand to his chest, pretending to be offended. While he was being overly dramatic, Rory stepped into the gap. "It's nice to meet you. It seems like you can handle the most important part of the job." She lifted her beer bottle in Bill's direction and said, "Putting up with him." Maggie and Lou laughed. Bill pretended to look shocked again.

"I would never have introduced you if I'd known you were going to gang up on me like this."

"What do you expect, Bill? You put a bunch of lesbians together, and we're either going to start a softball team or have a potluck. Or make fun of you." Lou grinned at him and patted him on the arm.

"That's it, I'm out of here." He turned and walked away, but not before stroking Lou on the shoulder in a reassuring way.

"Did you bring a date?"

"Rory, that's none of our business. Forgive her crassness—she's just a romantic at heart and wants to make sure everyone is in love." Maggie smiled affectionately at her wife and Rory kissed her on the forehead.

For a moment, Lou envied them their easy affection. But she quickly admonished herself. She knew their current state of comfort hadn't come easy, and they had each paid a price. But they seemed to be making it work. The love she saw passing between them assured her that they would end the evening in each other's arms. Shaking herself out of her reverie, she realized she hadn't answered Rory's question. "No, I had one, but I canceled it."

Rory looked disappointed for her. "Oh, I'm sorry to hear that." Suddenly, something over Lou's shoulder caught her attention and she said, "Well, looks like you might be in luck. Looks like that gorgeous blonde over there is checking you out. She seems really interested." Rory grinned and inclined her head. She lifted her bottle in the air to the woman in question and nodded her head.

Maggie put her hand on Rory's arm. "Rory..." But she shook her head, laughing.

Lou turned in the direction Rory was looking, hoping she wasn't going to see who she expected, but sure enough, there was Steve, and she was walking toward her with a look of determination. Steve was just as dashing as she had been on their first date. Why did she have to clean up so nice, Lou wondered. *Focus*—the problem wasn't her looks or her charm, dammit.

When Steve reached them, she nodded briefly to Rory and Maggie but she was lasered in on Lou. "Can we go somewhere and talk?"

"Steve, I do want to talk to you, but I don't want to be rude." She gestured vaguely to Rory and Maggie, who were doing their best to politely ignore them.

"Oh no, you two go on. We're fine here," Rory assured them.

Lou nodded to Rory and gave her a quick smile. She saw what Rory was up to. It was hard to miss the note of mischief on her face. She might have enjoyed it on any other day, but she just wasn't in the mood to deal with the whole Steve issue right now, so it was hard to see the humor in what appeared to be Rory's well-intentioned meddling.

"See, they're fine. I just need a few minutes, Lou. Please?"

It was hard to turn away from the pleading she saw on Steve's face, but she couldn't handle it. "Not now, Steve." She turned and walked away from her, not going anywhere in particular, just away. The party was well under way and the house was full of guests, and she had to dodge several people she didn't know on her way through the house. She knew Steve was following her and she wasn't sure how she felt about that. At one point, she stopped and smiled to herself. Maybe she liked it all right. She made her way to the door that led to the backyard and stepped out onto Bill and Dix's patio. No one else was out, since it was too cold for most people, but Lou enjoyed it. She hugged her arms to herself as she leaned against the side of the house and looked up at the stars.

From behind her she heard, "There's our girl up there now, looking as beautiful as ever." Steve walked a few steps closer to her, her dress shoes tap-tapping on the brick patio.

Lou turned and Steve was pointing up to the heavens, her finger indicating Cassiopeia. Lou turned back around and looked where Steve indicated. "Yep, there she is. Just as beautiful as ever, but I wouldn't say that too loud. You don't want to stroke her ego too much."

Steve chuckled. "No. Nighttime ego check."

"I don't think she'd take too kindly to me smacking her on the chest."

"No, probably not. Lou, we need to discuss this."

Lou turned to face her. Her face was an unreadable mask. She said very calmly, "I know."

"Then why'd you run away from me in there?"

"Just because I know we need to have this conversation, that doesn't mean I'm ready for it."

"That makes two of us." Steve stood only a few inches away from her and kept her hands in her pockets. She wanted to reach out to Lou, but she didn't want to frighten her off.

Lou sighed. "Steve, there's a part of me that wants to just kiss you right now and keep kissing you until the song plays. There's another part of me that just wants to shake your hand and wish you a nice life, because I don't know if we can get through our baggage enough to have a relationship together."

"I know. And there's a part of me that wants to pull you to me for that kiss and keep kissing you until it's not today anymore. Then the other, more sensible side just wants to apologize profusely, hope you forgive me, and wish you well."

Lou took one small step toward Steve but didn't reach out. "Sometimes I hate being an adult, but I think it's for the best."

"Yeah."

"Soldier, you came in and swept me off my feet, you romanced me and charmed me, and it was wonderful. But you also made me take a look at myself, closer than I ever have before, and I wasn't happy with what I saw, not all of it. I'm working on those things now. I'm trying to learn how to forgive and to let go of my anger, but it's going to take time. I don't know if I can be with someone while I go through this. I'm sorry for hurting you, for shutting you out. But my love is real. Can we revisit this on another day? If it's not too late by then?" Lou looked at Steve, and in her face Steve saw hope, but fear.

Steve searched her face for clues to what she was thinking, but she just wasn't sure. Finally, she heaved a heavy sigh, accepting defeat. "Losing you is what hurts, but I get what you're saying. We will revisit this on another day." Steve offered her hand to shake and Lou put her hand in hers. But instead of shaking, Steve bowed slightly and brought Lou's fingers to her lips and kissed them. When she stood she saw the tears beginning to form in Lou's eyes, as she was sure they were in hers. She said, "It won't be too late."

Lou left her hand in Steve's for a moment, then awkwardly

pulled it back and turned without a word and went back into the house. She wiped her eyes as she went.

Steve took a few steps across the patio, then looked up at the sky and saw the brightest star of the night shining brilliantly, just as she heard the countdown begin from inside. She muttered to herself, "*Beneath the rage of burning Sirius rise…*" She stopped, not because she didn't remember the rest, but because she did not share Homer's dread. Instead, she pulled her eyes away from the heavens and said, "You're wrong, Homer, it's not an evil portent." Steve turned and hurried back inside, through the room full of revelers. Everyone was hugging and kissing and dancing in the new year. In all the revelry, it took her a moment to spot Lou, walking away from Bill and Dix toward the door. Steve pushed past the partiers until she was by Lou's side. When she was next to her, she reached out and lightly touched Lou's arm. Lou turned around, curious. When she saw who was behind her, she was obviously repressing a smile.

"Lou, before you go…I just had to say that it's a new day, and I hope it's not too late. I mean, we both have stuff to work through, but work always goes faster with two people instead of one, you know?" Steve felt like she was bungling it and seeing Lou biting her lip to keep from laughing was a sure sign that she was. "What I mean is, I love you, Lou, and I want to start the rest of our lives right now."

Lou couldn't hold back the giggle and she covered her mouth. "Did you watch *When Harry Met Sally* last night?"

Steve grinned. "Well, it sounded much better when he said it." Steve took a step closer to Lou, who was now smiling, and caressed her cheek, then leaned in for a slow kiss. Lou's arms went around her neck, and Steve kissed her with more passion.

After several moments, Lou pulled away and looked Steve in the eyes. "You're getting much better at reading signals, soldier."

"You wanted me to come after you, didn't you?"

Lou nodded. "I was really hoping you would."

"What if I hadn't?"

"Then, I guess, I would have had to turn around and go back out to the patio and just grab you and give you the kiss of your life."

"You can still do that."

"You make an excellent point." Lou pulled Steve to her and did indeed give her the kiss of her life. Steve was gasping when she let her go.

"Thank God this worked, or I might have had to stand outside your window holding a boom box or go to that café of yours and sing 'You've Lost That Loving Feeling.' "

"Just how many eighties movies did you watch last night?"

"All of them, I watched all the movies." Steve grinned at her, then kissed the top of her forehead.

"It's probably a good thing my parents are gone," Lou noted. "That way you don't have to do a big dance number in front of them to prove your love for me."

"You are horrible." But she was laughing.

Before they could laugh or kiss any more, Bill came up to them and said, "No one puts Louie in the corner."

Instead of acknowledging his use of her childhood nickname, something she had never told him about, she admonished him instead. "Bill, you were eavesdropping."

"Of course I was—I had to make sure you two didn't screw this up. I'm just trying to keep the family together." Bill put a hand on each of their shoulders and smiled at each of them in turn. "I'm guessing you two crazy kids are going to work this out?"

"Yep. One day at a time." Lou smiled at them both.

"Now there was a good show," Steve said.

"Steve, honey, I feel you're getting sidetracked," Lou teased as Bill drifted away again.

"You're right. Would you like to get out of here and take a moonlit stroll? I know this great place where you can see the stars."

"That sounds wonderful. Maybe I can show you others besides you know who."

Steve pulled out her necklace from under her shirt and kissed it before letting it fall back to her chest. Then she smiled at Lou and said, "I would like that very much. Let's go. Show me the stars, Lou." She stepped back and held out her arm and Lou took it with a smile, and they left Bill and Dix's place and made their way to Lake Van Horn, where Lou showed Steve more stars and they kissed under the watchful gaze of the envious moon and the vain queen.

Chapter Twenty-Five

So, what does the *Farmers' Almanac* say about New Year's?" Steve asked, as she cuddled Lou to her as they lay on top of the covers on her bed, where they had come after strolling around the lake. They were both still in their party clothes but had kicked their shoes off inside the living room door, and Steve had hung her suit jacket up before they got comfortable. Her only other deference to comfort had been to untie her tie. She was sitting back against her pillows cradling Lou to her chest.

Lou smiled at the question as she lazily fingered Steve's tie. "Nothing that I recall, but it's been a while since I've read one. Other than Sirius, the only other thing I know about New Year's Eve is that it's tradition to eat black-eyed peas. But I didn't need the *Farmers' Almanac* to tell me that, my grandmother did. She was from Virginia. Made them every year. They're supposed to bring good luck."

"I've heard that. We never ate them in my house, though. In my house, we stayed up late on New Year's watching scary movies and eating popcorn and all kinds of other bad, delicious things."

Lou chuckled. "Why scary movies?"

"Because it was fun to critique them. Dad made a game out of counting how many jump scares there were. We laughed every time one came up. We made the mistake of going to see a scary movie at the theater once and everyone looked at us funny when we laughed while the rest of them screamed. We just watched scary movies at home after that."

Lou put her head on Steve's chest, laughing. When she came up for air, she said, "Oh my God, I love your family."

"Well, my family loves you." Steve grew melancholy. "I just wish you could have met my dad. He was the best." A smile of remembrance flashed across Steve's face and she wasn't there for a moment.

"Would your dad have liked me?" Lou asked with real concern.

"Are you kidding? He would have insisted that you call him Dad and immediately dubbed you an Adams. Then he would have given you a role—like, on Christmas every year it would be your job to decorate the tree or hand out presents or something. That's how he welcomed you. Well that, and big hugs every time he saw you. My dad was a teddy bear. And he gave great hugs." Steve hugged Lou tighter.

Steve's embrace made her smile, as did the picture Steve had just created for her in her mind. Her father had been a teddy bear too, once. She remembered when she was small enough to sit on his shoulders. He would put her up there saying, "Climb up on me so you can be closer to the stars." She would eagerly run to him and be lifted up, and it felt so high. Her little legs would go around his neck and he would take her hands in his. Then he would proceed to tell her and her mother stories about the stars, most of which she couldn't remember from that time. But since he often retold the same stories, she eventually learned them all, and later, after she was old enough to read and understand books, she would add to his stories with stories of her own. Once he had asked her how she knew so much, and she had replied, "I learned from the best."

A tear escaped her and she tried to surreptitiously wipe it away, but Steve noticed her movement.

"Oh, honey, I'm sorry. I should have realized. No more

stories." Steve tightened her arms around Lou and kissed her on top of her head, cupping her cheek in her hand.

"No, that's okay. I like hearing them. And that was a happy memory. I promise."

"You sure?"

"Yes, baby, I'm sure. I've worked hard over the years to hold on to them. I don't want to forget that I did once have a good father. It wasn't his fault what happened to him, but he chose to not seek help for it. I don't want to be like him in that regard." Lou leaned back out of Steve's embrace a bit so she could look up at her. "I mean, I'm proud to have his tenacity when it comes to certain things. And I credit my career to him, in part. If he hadn't taught me all about different weapons and such, who knows where my love of theater would have taken me. Probably just writing." Steve was smiling at her and she realized she was babbling, so she decided to say only one more thing on the subject. "I'm going to get help for my past trauma."

"I'm glad."

Lou slipped a leg over Steve's and looked up at her with a smile. "And I want a future with you, soldier. One that doesn't involve anger and violence."

"Couldn't agree more."

"But that doesn't mean tickling's off the table." Lou rolled on top of Steve and began tickling her sides and anywhere else she could reach.

Steve squealed but quickly got the upper hand and rolled Lou on her back. Their tickles quickly turned to playful kisses, and Steve's tie got thrown to the floor. Just as Lou was in the process of playfully biting her on the neck, Steve pulled back with a note of surprised comprehension in her voice, "Sirius! The Dog Star! That's why Rowling named him that!"

Lou burst out laughing. "You are such a dork."

"What? It just came to me."

"Uh-huh."

"It did!"

With a smile on her face, Lou replied, "Je t'aime, tu dork."
Steve growled low in her throat. "Ah, Lou, French!" Steve took hold of Lou's hand and began to kiss up Lou's arm, which just made Lou giggle more.

When Steve's kisses reached Lou's lips, their mutual giggles subsided. Lou put her arms around Steve's neck and met her lips with hers for a soft, sweet kiss.

About the Author

T.L. Hayes (http://TLHayesweb.com) is just your typical overeducated, underemployed dyke in the process of starting new journeys. She has held many jobs, including customer service agent, housekeeper, and poll-taker. None of them has been as satisfying as writing, especially writing stories with predominantly gay characters. She holds master's degrees in English and educational studies, and an incredible amount of student loan debt. She has recently moved back to her home state of Illinois and is enjoying all four seasons again.

Books Available From Bold Strokes Books

A Fighting Chance by T. L. Hayes. Will Lou be able to come to terms with her past to give love a fighting chance? (978-1-163555-257-7)

Chosen by Brey Willows. When the choice is adapt or die, can love save us all? (978-1-163555-110-5)

Gnarled Hollow by Charlotte Greene. After they are invited to study a secluded nineteenth-century estate, a former English professor and a group of historians discover that they will have to fight against the unknown if they have any hope of staying alive. (978-1-163555-235-5)

Jacob's Grace by C.P. Rowlands. Captain Tag Becket wants to keep her head down and her past behind her, but her feelings for AJ's second-in-command, Grace Fields, makes keeping secrets next to impossible. (978-1-163555-187-7)

On the Fly by PJ Trebelhorn. Hockey player Courtney Abbott is content with her solitary life until visiting concert violinist Lana Caruso makes her second-guess everything she always thought she wanted. (978-1-163555-255-3)

Passionate Rivals by Radclyffe. Professional rivalry and long-simmering passions create a combustible combination when Emmet McCabe and Sydney Stevens are forced to work together, especially when past attractions won't stay buried. (978-1-63555-231-7)

Proxima Five by Missouri Vaun. When geologist Leah Warren crash-lands on a preindustrial planet and is claimed by its tyrant, Tiago, will clan warrior Keegan's love for Leah give her the strength to defeat him? (978-1-163555-122-8)

Racing Hearts by Dena Blake. When you cross a hot-tempered race car mechanic with a reckless cop, the result can only be spontaneous combustion. (978-1-163555-251-5)

Shadowboxer by Jessica L. Webb. Jordan McAddie is prepared to keep her street kids safe from a dangerous underground protest group, but she isn't prepared for her first love to walk back into her life. (978-1-163555-267-6)

The Tattered Lands by Barbara Ann Wright. As Vandra and Lilani strive to make peace, they slowly fall in love. With mistrust and murder surrounding them, only their faith in each other can keep their plan to save the world from falling apart. (978-1-163555-108-2)

Captive by Donna K. Ford. To escape a human trafficking ring, Greyson Cooper and Olivia Danner become players in a game of deceit and violence. Will their love stand a chance? (978-1-63555-215-7)

Crossing the Line by CF Frizzell. The Mob discovers a nemesis within its ranks, and in the ultimate retaliation, draws Stick McLaughlin from anonymity by threatening everything she holds dear. (978-1-63555-161-7)

Love's Verdict by Carsen Taite. Attorneys Landon Holt and Carly Pachett want the exact same thing: the only open partnership spot at their prestigious criminal defense firm. But will they compromise their careers for love? (978-1-63555-042-9)

Precipice of Doubt by Mardi Alexander & Laurie Eichler. Can Cole Jameson resist her attraction to her boss, veterinarian Jodi Bowman, or will she risk a workplace romance and her heart? (978-1-63555-128-0)

Savage Horizons by CJ Birch. Captain Jordan Kellow's feelings for Lt. Ali Ash have her past and future colliding, setting in motion a series of events that strands her crew in an unknown galaxy thousands of light years from home. (978-1-63555-250-8)

Secrets of the Last Castle by A. Rose Mathieu. When Elizabeth Campbell represents a young man accused of murdering an elderly woman, her investigation leads to an abandoned plantation that reveals many dark Southern secrets. (978-1-63555-240-9)

Take Your Time by VK Powell. A neurotic parrot brings police officer Grace Booker and temporary veterinarian Dr. Dani Wingate together in the tiny town of Pine Cone, but their unexpected attraction keeps the sparks flying. (978-1-63555-130-3)

The Last Seduction by Ronica Black. When you allow true love to elude you once and you desperately regret it, are you brave enough to grab it when it comes around again? (978-1-63555-211-9)

The Shape of You by Georgia Beers. Rebecca McCall doesn't play it safe, but when sexy Spencer Thompson joins her workout class, their nonstop sparring forces her to face her ultimate challenge—a chance at love. (978-1-63555-217-1)

Exposed by MJ Williamz. The closet is no place to live if you want to find true love. (978-1-62639-989-1)

Force of Fire: Toujours a Vous by Ali Vali. Immortals Kendal and Piper welcome their new child and celebrate the defeat of an old enemy, but another ancient evil is about to awaken deep in the jungles of Costa Rica. (978-1-63555-047-4)

Landing Zone by Erin Dutton. Can a career veteran finally discover a love stronger than even her pride? (978-1-63555-199-0)

Love at Last Call by M. Ullrich. Is balancing business, friendship, and love more than any willing woman can handle? (978-1-63555-197-6)

Pleasure Cruise by Yolanda Wallace. Spencer Collins and Amy Donovan have few things in common, but a Caribbean cruise offers both women an unexpected chance to face one of their greatest fears: falling in love. (978-1-63555-219-5)

Running Off Radar by MB Austin. Maji's plans to win Rose back are interrupted when work intrudes, and duty calls her to help a SEAL team stop a Russian mobster from harvesting gold from the bottom of Sitka Sound. (978-1-63555-152-5)

Shadow of the Phoenix by Rebecca Harwell. In the final battle for the fate of Storm's Quarry, even Nadya's and Shay's powers may not be enough. (978-1-63555-181-5)

Take a Chance by D. Jackson Leigh. There's hardly a woman within fifty miles of Pine Cone that veterinarian Trip Beaumont can't charm, except for the irritating new cop, Jamie Grant, who keeps leaving parking tickets on her truck. (978-1-63555-118-1)

Death in Time by Robyn Nyx. Working in the past is hell on your future. (978-1-63555-053-5)

The Outcasts by Alexa Black. Spacebus driver Sue Jones is running from her past. When she crash-lands on a faraway world, the Outcast Kara might be her chance for redemption. (978-1-63555-242-3)

Alias by Cari Hunter. A car crash leaves a woman with no memory and no identity. Together with Detective Bronwen Pryce, she fights to uncover a truth that might just kill them both. (978-1-63555-221-8)

Hers to Protect by Nicole Disney. Ex–high school sweethearts Kaia and Adrienne will have to see past their differences and survive the vengeance of a brutal gang if they want to be together. (978-1-63555-229-4)

Perfect Little Worlds by Clifford Mae Henderson. Lucy can't hold the secret any longer. Twenty-six years ago, her sister did the unthinkable. (978-1-63555-164-8)

Room Service by Fiona Riley. Interior designer Olivia likes stability, but when work brings footloose Savannah into her world and into a new city every month, Olivia must decide if what makes her comfortable is what makes her happy. (978-1-63555-120-4)

Sparks Like Ours by Melissa Brayden. Professional surfers Gia Malone and Elle Britton can't deny their chemistry on and off the beach. But only one can win… (978-1-63555-016-0)

Take My Hand by Missouri Vaun. River Hemsworth arrives in Georgia intent on escaping quickly, but when she crashes her Mercedes into the Clip 'n Curl, sexy Clay Cahill ends up rescuing more than her car. (978-1-63555-104-4)

The Last Time I Saw Her by Kathleen Knowles. Lane Hudson only has twelve days to win back Alison's heart. That is, if she can gather the courage to try. (978-1-63555-067-2)

Wayworn Lovers by Gun Brooke. Will agoraphobic composer Giselle Bonnaire and Tierney Edwards, a wandering soul who can't remain in one place for long, trust in the passionate love destiny hands them? (978-1-62639-995-2)